THE VICTIM KILLER

A SAM RADER THRILLER

SIMON KING

Your Free Books Are Waiting.
Get three exciting books right now absolutely free and start your journey into the thrilling world of Simon King at www. booksbysimonking.com

Grab Your Starter Library

FOREWORD

Welcome to the world of Samantha Rader and her introduction into a world filled with serial killers. The series is essentially a continuation from The Lawson Chronicles, although is also a standalone series that stands on its own merits.

To bring you up to speed and understand some of the facts that have shaped Sam into the person she is at the start of the series, I have included a letter she reads at the beginning of this book, labelled "A letter from Judith". You can find it at the end of this book, labelled, A Letter from Judith. It provides enough background information for you to fully enjoy the series from the very beginning, should you wish to read it.

Thank you
Simon

CONTENTS

THE VICTIM KILLER

1
_____

Samuel Rader watched as his daughter read the letter a second time, her eyes slowly darting from one line to the next. She was gripping it tight between her fingers, both hands holding it in her lap. Despite refusing to read it the first time he had offered it, shortly after Samantha's 15th birthday, the young woman now absorbed her mother's final words like an executor would the words of a client's final will and testament.

The small cottage sat silently around them, a small blessing when hidden high up in the mountains of the Mosquito Ranges. Jasper lay patiently at Samantha's feet as she read, the dog always happy when her friend returned home.

Samuel had almost forgotten about the letter entirely, having stuffed it away after the only time he'd offered it to her. That was 10 long years ago, and when Sam asked about it during a recent phone call, it took him a moment to recall what she'd meant. The letter; that final goodbye Judith had written for her daughter just before she ended her life. His own letter from her had been sitting beside Sam's, but he'd only needed to open his own. It explained everything he needed to know, including her apology for finally giving in to her demons.

Sam looked up from the letter, reached down and gave Jasper a pat. He looked up, his tail slowly swishing from side to side in anticipation of more attention. She didn't speak at first, giving the words a moment to sink in. The silence, now broken by a soft tail slowly sweeping back and forth, continued to hang heavy between them. Finally, Sam folded the note, stuffed it back into the envelope and handed it back to her father.

"You don't want to hang on to it, kiddo?" he asked, but Sam shook her head.

"No. Not yet."

"Did you find the answers you were looking for?" Sam pondered the question, looked out towards the small window and slowly nodded.

"Did she really die like that? Her mom, I mean?"

"Apparently so. She didn't talk about it much. There was one time where a man called Jim Lawson came to visit and they briefly spoke of that moment. I think it was more for my benefit than theirs. I guess sometimes it's easier just to pretend you can run away from such memories."

"Do you think that's what *I've* been doing?" Jasper stood and laid his head on Sam's lap. She stroked between his ears the way that always made him freeze and enjoy the moment.

"You? Run? Sweetheart, the only time you run is *towards* an issue. Don't ever think that. There's a reason-"

"...the past is behind you, yes I remember," Sam finished, her father's favorite saying also finishing her mom's letter, like a final piece of guiding advice.

"She struggled with her memories for a very long time. Childhood trauma will do that to a person. But her biggest fear was that *you* would somehow inherit the same trauma."

"But isn't that what happened?" She looked at her father

with accusing eyes, as if he somehow had something to do with it. But Samuel only smiled gently back at her.

"You may have some of the traits your mom tried to protect you from, but you also have more mental strength than I have ever seen in anybody. And now your FBI training as well? Kid, if anyone can beat this, it's you."

Samuel reached forward and squeezed her shoulder. She had been "training" since her 10th birthday, courtesy of an over-protective, ex-navy-seal father. He knew that whatever internal struggles she faced, there was no-one more qualified to handle them. He'd often wondered whether her internal strength had already surpassed his own.

Sam looked at him then, in a way he hadn't seen in a very long time. There was a fear in her eyes that reminded him of a time when he knew he had to help her. The whole mess with the kid at school. But that had been more than a decade ago. She'd grown so much since then.

"I just...," but her words stopped, unable to continue. The letter had possibly answered more of her questions than she was expecting. How easy is it to learn that a prolific serial killer had taken your mom hostage and made her take part in some of his atrocities? Harry Lightman had been a constant nightmare for Judith for decades before she finally gave in. Samuel wondered just how much further the ramifications would travel. Would they eventually consume Samantha as well?

"If there is one thing I'm certain of, is that you will never give up. We will beat this together, you hear me?" Sam stood, gave her father a hug and closed her eyes. The voice inside her mind always quietened when he was near, as if afraid, knowing that he would do everything in his power to silence it once and for all if he could.

After giving her father a final hug later that afternoon, Sam headed back down the mountain, reaching the town of Fairplay a little after four. The rental she'd hired at Denver airport had been one of the last available, the small Toyota slowly eating the miles to get her back in time for her 6 o'clock flight. With luck, she would step into her apartment a little after 9.

Kansas City had been her second choice when trainees were given the option, the Denver FBI field office her first. But when she received the notice, advising her that the building she would shortly call home was located only a short flight from her home, Sam knew she was one of the lucky ones. People didn't always get a preference. One of her classmates at Quantico had been transferred to California, despite her family living in Florida.

After briefly stopping at a 7/11 and topping up with gas for the car and a Coke for herself, Sam settled into the short drive back to Denver. As she watched the traffic pass by, her mind wandered back to the letter, the final goodbye that had been waiting for her since her mother's suicide. The letter had answered a lot more than her father imagined, because the urges he only suspected her of having, were not only real, but also intensifying.

Her mom had known about them, because she herself had had them as well. The urge to feel blood running between her fingers, its warm stickiness begging her to continue seeking it; to taste the coppery sweetness and feel the warmth slowly trickle down her throat.

Sam closed her eyes, desperate to push the thoughts aside. She held the steering wheel taut, feeling the tires gently vibrate as they continued to travel along the highway. She opened her eyes again and saw the first spots of what would soon turn into a late afternoon thunderstorm.

After switching the wiper blades on, Sam reached for the Coke and took a long sip, holding the liquid in her mouth as if to gargle it like mouthwash. The drink felt cool, but thirst was not what she was trying to quench. The soda washed the imaginary taste of blood from her mouth, replacing it with something she recognized. Coke had been her first drink after that very first incident when she was just 9. It was that very incident she had been expecting to read about in the letter, but her mother had died before that day, the timeline sometimes a little more hazy than she wanted.

Forcing the thoughts from her mind, Sam switched on the car's radio, played with the dials for a few moments, then settled back in her seat as Freddie Mercury exploded out of the speakers with "Radio Ga Ga". Queen had always been one of her favorites and now did what she hoped it would. Her mind soon turned back to her destination and why she needed to get back to Kansas City, her first day of work now less than 15 hours away.

The lines at the airport were minimal and after returning her car and clearing check in, Sam was soon waiting for the plane to start taxiing. The flight was far from full and she had the fortune of having the entire row to herself.

The rain had turned almost torrential whilst she was still a half hour from Denver, but after that initial downfall, it had settled into a regular shower that looked to remain for the time being. As Sam looked out of the plane's window, rain pattered the glass, running down in faint lines.

As the plane slowly began to move beneath her, she felt a sense of relief wash over her. Soon, she would be airborne, headed towards a new future that would give her something to focus on, other than the urges. Because if they ever really took hold, she knew the chances of stopping them would be almost impossible.

Sam hadn't flown often, but each time she did, found it to be incredibly somnific. Before the plane had climbed to its cruising altitude, the young woman was already fast asleep, the air hostess simply smiling at her as she passed during service. But if the young stewardess knew what the passenger was dreaming, there would have been no smile. For the horror that sometimes returned from the past, also brought with it the emotional freight train that followed after those events; events that had changed this woman's life forever.

Julie Temple had only one purpose in life, 9-year old Samantha believed. And that was to make her life a living hell. Although she had heard the term "bully" a number of times whilst listening to teachers softly whispering above her, it wasn't a term that seemed to fit the torment she endured almost daily.

The pair had first met the previous year when Julie had moved into their neighborhood. But things went bad almost immediately when Sam had shown Julie her collection of "pets", dead insects and small animals she'd hidden in a box out behind the garden shed.

The name calling began shortly after, Julie relentlessly turning classmates against the socially awkward Sam within days. The bullying continued for months before Samuel caught wind of it. But even he couldn't bring an end to it, just like the teachers, or the parents. None believed sweet Julie capable of such atrocious behavior. The abuse continued until one fateful morning when everything changed.

Sam had walked to her locker during the morning break and found the word "Freakazoid" written across the door in thick black marker. As she stood in front of it, staring at the horrible name, she heard a snickering from somewhere further down the hallway. When Sam turned to see where it came from, she saw Julie Temple standing beside a large group of girls, all staring at her.

Some were whispering to each other behind hands, while others were laughing and pointing. It would have never escalated if Julie didn't step forward then, calling for the freakazoid to show them her little pet cemetery.

"See Hailey here? Her new kitten went missing. Did you steal him, Freakazoid? Steal him and add him to your freaky zoo?" Sam could feel her cheeks burning, hoping for the ground to swallow her up. She turned away, opened her locker door and tried her best to ignore the unwanted attention.

But the more she tried to ignore them, the more they made themselves heard. Julie began to chant "Freak" over and over again, waving her hands up and up to entice the rest of her crew to join in. They did, slowly walking forward as their rhythmic chanting filled the air around the lonely girl standing before them.

More people joined in as the chanting carried through the corridor with a near-deafening echo of abuse. Most had no idea what the yelling was about, simply wanting to join in with whatever was happening. With the crowd less than 10 yards from where Sam was standing, it looked as if they were about to set upon her.

Maybe they would have, had it not been for Mr. Holtz, who happened to walk past on his way to the school gymnasium.

"Vhat iz going on here?" he yelled in his thick German accent. When he didn't break through the instant chanting, he blew his whistle until the last of the kids had stopped yelling, then told everyone to get to class. But if Sam believed things to be over for the day, she was wrong, because lunchtime turned out to be even worse.

This time the group followed their victim into the girl's

toilets. Julie had grown in confidence since the earlier episode and now figured she could get physical with the smaller girl. Her 6 friends followed their self-imposed leader, keen to see what else she had in store for the freak.

Sam had left her bag outside of the cubicle and Julie pounced on it almost the second she walked in.

"Oh, what have we here?" she cooed, unzipping the small backpack. A library book was the first item to be pulled out of the bag. Julie tore the book in half and flung the two pieces over the stall door, to which her friends nervously chuckled. They knew there was a line and Julie looked to be crossing it.

Inside the stall, Sam anxiously sat on the edge of the toilet, her knees tucked in tight to her chest. She jumped a little as Julie began to bang on the door, calling for her to come out. Next came her lunch, first a squished ham and cheese sandwich, which bounced off her head and splashed into the toilet bowl beneath.

"Come out, you fucken coward," Julie yelled and the others paused at hearing the "F" word. "Come out or I'll send Reggie here, in to get you." Julie banged the door, then kicked her foot underneath it to highlight how easily someone could slide under and into the cubicle. And that was when it happened. Julie was about to cross a line even her friends would later say was too far.

"Bet your mom killed herself because of your freakiness."

Sam suddenly felt an overwhelming sense of rage. At first, she thought simply waiting the girls out would fix things. Lunchtime only went for another 30 minutes and she was sure she could sit inside the cubicle and wait for her tormentors to grow tired and leave.

But hearing her mom mentioned tipped her over the edge. A switch flicked something on inside her and she jumped off the toilet, unlocked the cubicle door and swung it open, facing her tormentor for the final time.

The girls stood behind Julie, blocking the exit. Sam had her back to the wall, waiting for her abuser to give the final push needed to cross the threshold.

"Is that what happened, bitch? Did your poor momma-"

But that was as far as she got. Sam reached forward, grabbed a handful of Julie's hair and pulled the girl off balance. The bigger girl first thought she had the size to make small work of the little pipsqueak, but when she felt herself pulled so suddenly, began to doubt herself.

The pair half-circled each other, Julie waving an arm about, trying to find her attacker's hair, but Sam kept her head back far enough to avoid the grasping fingers. The rage felt like burning heat inside her, thoughts of anger and pain eclipsing everything else from her mind.

"BITCH!" Julie screamed, launching a kick that caught Sam in the shin. The pain barely registered with her intended target, who swung her own shoe back in a retaliatory strike. "FREAKAZOID BITCH!"

That was when Sam reached out with her foot and tangled it between Julie's desperate legs. They jittered together for a brief second, then crashed onto the bathroom's tiled floor. The other girls simply stood their ground, mouths open, unable to move. It was after a few seconds of wrestling that Julie made her final mistake, one she would regret for the rest of her life.

Sam was getting the better of her, working her way around to lying on top of her abuser. One hand was still firmly entangled in a mop of long hair, while the other had grabbed the collar on the girl's shirt. Julie was trying desperately to buck her off, but her efforts continued to be in vain as her anguish and frustration grew. And that was when she said the words that would push a delicately balanced Samantha completely over the edge.

"NO WONDER YOUR BITCH MOTHER KILLED HERSELF!"

Everything paused at that moment. The girls standing above them let out a uniformed "ahhhh" of shock. Sam pulled her face back slightly and looked into the face of her tormentor, a look of overwhelming wrath building behind her eyes that had portrayed grief and anger only moments before. This rage was different; turning the world into a dark shade of red.

Sam briefly screamed, then launched herself into Julie's face. A second later blood filled her mouth, warm and sticky, seeming to fuel her boiling rage further like gasoline poured on a camp fire. Her teeth sank into the soft flesh of cheek, the now terrified girl unable to shake her attacker free.

As the blood began to spatter around them, the entourage took a few steps back, their friend's screams continuing to rise in an operatic crescendo. Blood pools were forming in several spots, Sam continuing to gnash her teeth into her abuser's face.

It was only after the girls ran from the toilet block screaming, that help finally arrived. 2 teachers, one of which was Mr. Holtz. His office was just across the way and he heard the frantic cries. By the time he finally made it into the cubicle, one girl's head looked like it had been dipped in blood, the sticky mess matting her long hair together like dread locks.

When they finally managed to separate the wrestling duo, one girl had a hole the size of a golf ball missing from her cheek. The damage was deep enough to show a neat row of blood-stained teeth beneath and Holtz would later say that he thought the girl had somehow used one of those temporary tattoos on her face.

But the injury was no illusion, the piece of missing meat lying on the tiled floor in a pool of bright blood nearby. The injured girl had stopped screaming, looking deathly white at her attacker with eyes as big as saucers. Sam stood, watching the other teacher. Mrs. Lewis looked almost as white as the injured girl herself, as she bent to help Julie up.

An ambulance would later take the young girl to hospital, a

small paper towel holding her missing piece of cheek in her lap. But the damage to the flesh had been severe and no doctor would ever reattach it to her face. The scar from that day would remain as a constant reminder of what happens when a victim of bullying finally snaps.

Samuel Rader was called in by the school principal and after a very brief meeting, left with his little girl by his side. He had been asked not to return her until "she had the necessary mental help she so clearly needed". That was the last day Samantha Rader ever attended school.

The drive home was almost in silence, Sam sitting beside her father, staring as the streets passed them by. It was only when they reached the town's limits that her father finally spoke.

"Is this seat taken?"

"Ma'am? Is this seat taken?" Sam slowly opened her eyes to find a man standing in the aisle beside her. "Miss?" It took her a few moments to remember where she was, the curtain of sleep slowly lifting as the passenger smiled down at her.

"No, sorry. I didn't realize anyone was sitting there."

"Thank you, Miss Rader," he said, sitting beside her, once Sam moved her handbag.

"How do you know my name?" she asked, watching him more intently. The stranger took a moment to slide a magazine into the storage pouch in front of him and turned to her again.

"We don't have a lot of time. The flight is due to start its descent soon." He ignored her question, looking past Sam and out through the tiny window behind her. Darkness stared back with only small scatterings of lights beneath them

"How do you know my name?" Sam repeated, feeling her nerves kick up a notch.

"We know a lot about you, Sam. May I call you Sam?" He fidgeted with the armrest as he spoke, almost as if he had his own nerves to contend with.

The man wore a dark suit, with a distinctive black and red tie. He couldn't have been older than 30, Sam thought to herself. It crossed her mind that he may have been testing her in preparation for the next day's activities. Maybe he was FBI, sent to follow their latest Special Agent around to see if she had any dark secrets hidden in her closet.

"I'm not FBI," he said, as if reading her mind. "The organization I work for is a little more low-key than them."

"Your organization?"

"We call ourselves 'Pogrom', but you won't find us mentioned in any official documentation. We're what you might call "a final solution" to many of the country's underlying problems."

"I don't follow," Sam said. He pulled a business card from his pocket and held it out to her. For a moment Sam stared at it. "I'm starting with the FBI tomorrow morning."

"Yes, I know. But you don't belong there, do you?"

"Belong there?"

"There's a lot you don't know about, Sam. There are a lot of questions you ask yourself daily, questions I asked myself a long time ago. You *are* one of us, although you mightn't know it yet." He held the card up a little higher. "This here? This is the answer you seek."

Unsure of why her fingers were trembling, Sam reached out and took the card. As her fingers closed around it, the seat belt sign suddenly chimed on above her.

The man grabbed his magazine from the pouch and stood. He turned back to her and bent his head slightly, the faint smell of cinnamon from his cologne reminding Sam of hot donuts.

"You don't belong there, Sam," he repeated. "Come and see us once you realize the FBI isn't your home."

He turned and walked back down the aisle as a flight attendant approached them. Sam looked at the business card, expecting to find a phone number and address, maybe even her new acquaintance's name. But all she found was a symbol, one she recognized instantly.

The M and W logo of Milton Ward stared back at her. He was a billionaire who's head office was in Kansas City and she immediately wondered whether they had somehow manipulated her FBI placement. There were no addresses or phone numbers, the reverse side of the card a simple mirror image of the front. The electronics giant had featured heavily in recent years for their revolutionary cell phones, the distinct logo always engraved into the back of them.

"Ma'am, seat belt sign is on," a voice suddenly said above her. She looked up to see the flight attendant looking down at her.

"Sorry," Sam said, dropping the card into her pocket before clipping the seat belt ends together. Once she made sure her passenger complied, the flight attendant continued walking down the aisle, looking down at each of the passengers in turn.

While the plane continued to descend towards Sam's new home, she wondered whether the man was real and the card was some kind of job invitation. She'd worked extremely hard to get to where she was and wasn't about to walk away from years of study and effort.

By the time the plane touched down in Kansas City, Samantha Rader had made up her mind to continue with what she set out to do. Whatever Milton Ward wanted from her, would have to take a back seat. Because the FBI was calling her and there was no way she was giving that up.

She didn't see the stranger again, either while she disembarked with the passengers, or during the long walk back to the main terminal. It was as if he'd never been there in the first place. But he had, Sam feeling the card in her pocket, as if to confirm it to herself.

As she walked, the man's words continued to repeat in her mind, his warning that she didn't belong with the FBI almost scaring her. The training at Quantico had not been easy for her and the effort it had taken to graduate was something she couldn't just walk away from. And yet his words also intrigued her somehow.

"You don't belong there," Sam whispered under her breath as she entered the main terminal. The crowds were thick, people jostling past her from all directions. This was Kansas City, her new home. And despite the man's attempts to put doubt in her mind, Sam would continue with her ambitions, just as she had planned to do for the past 5 years.

She continued to head towards the exit doors at the other side of the building. The eyes that were intently watching her from a nearby alcove, focused on the intended recruit, a recruit that possessed the specific qualities that made Pogrom such a unique venture, a venture that ended lives.

2

Sam didn't sleep soundly that night, the hours passing with a monotonous drag that felt to go on forever. The sounds of her apartment, still new to the young graduate, felt as foreign as the constant sounds of civilization from outside her window. City life had not come easy to a girl born and raised in the country, many miles from her nearest neighbors.

The man returned to her thoughts again and again, his cleanly-shaven smile, the warmth-filled eyes looking back at her. Had he been real? Anything felt possible in the small hours of the morning, when reason and common sense hid in the shadows of nightfall.

But he had been real, the card still in her purse. She'd looked at it in the elevator, then again as she ate a late snack before bed. A plain white card, glistening with the shininess of a new car, a single symbol staring back like an all-seeing eye.

Now lying in bed and tossing and turning from one side to the other as sleep completely eluded her, Sam wondered why a billionaire would be interested in her. Milton Ward had made his fortune in electronics, the media often labelling him as the new Steve Jobs. With his impressive array of cutting-edge consumer products, the people quickly turned his latest products into instant household names, often purchasing hundreds of thousands of units upon release.

It didn't make sense and it was that very puzzle that kept her awake, unable to settle the questions in her mind enough to slip into sleep. No matter how hard she tried to switch her thinking to something else, the man kept returning, until at one point, Milton Ward himself was standing beside him, the pair of them holding out a hand to her.

Sam desperately tried to sleep, aware of how important the next day would be. She needed rest, and it wasn't until she turned her mind back to her mother's final letter, that she finally began to relax. Within a few minutes of thinking about the words written on that paper, she slipped into the fog, sleep welcoming her with open arms.

"Special Agent Rader, you are late. That's not a good start. Tardiness won't be tolerated on my floor, do you understand?" Samantha felt the heat rise in her cheeks as she stood before a man almost half as large as the desk he was sitting behind. Nathan Watson stared back at her over the top of his tiny reading glasses, like an annoyed librarian. The noise that had filled the large office only a moment before, now felt to quieten as the rest of the agents stopped to listen in.

"Sorry, sir. I had a-"

"And excuses are totally irrelevant when you stroll into your new job 11 minutes after the time you should have been standing right where you are now. JORVINSKI!" Sam looked behind her and saw a man stand from a desk near the back of the room. "This is Agent Jorvinski. Listen to him and learn. And

The Victim Killer

don't let me see you late again." He waved her away as if swatting some fly from his dinner plate.

Jorvinski beckoned for Sam to follow him and she did, grateful that the noise level once again increased to its former volumes. Once out in the hallway, he turned back to her, offering his hand.

"Tim Jorvinski. Don't mind him, he just gets a little rambunctious with all the new agents."

"Sam Rader." The pair shook, but somehow the introduction felt weak to Sam, almost forced.

"Let me give you a tour of the place and then get you settled in at your own desk. Coffee?" he offered, pointing at an instant vending machine. She shook her head, but Jorvinski dropped the coins in and pressed the button as other agents continued to pass them.

"It's a lot busier than I expected," she offered while they waited.

"This? This is nothing. Wait till the afternoon shift arrives. Then you'll wonder how the floor keeps everybody up."

Once the cup was retrieved, Tim continued the tour, showing Samantha around 5 of the building's 37 floors. Although he introduced her to almost a dozen people, none felt warm and inviting to Sam, most just offering her a forced smile before returning their attention to whatever importance was displayed on their computer screens.

The entire tour took around an hour and by the time Sam was seated at what was to become her own work station, her mind had wandered back to the man from the plane.

"You don't belong there," he had told her and she wondered for the first time if he was right. She didn't feel welcomed here and as she thought back to her first day at Quantico, remembered a similar feeling back then.

At the time, Sam had put down her uncomfortable apprehension to just nerves, experienced by anybody who's ever started at a new school or work placement. That same sense of nervous tension had followed her for weeks during training and now seemed to have re-risen here in Kansas City.

Tim had given Sam some files of current homicide cases, as well as her log-in details to the central database. He wanted her to scan the cases and familiarize herself with them as she would be working them in the coming weeks. Once he saw she was successfully logged in with the first file open, he returned to his own side of the desk, their workstations butted up against each other. Sam picked up the first folder and began to read.

Just before 12, a man came into the large office and began to call out names. As each person answered, they walked up and were handed a small bag containing either sandwiches or some other form of lunch. There were drinks handed out as well and as Tim returned from getting his own, offered Sam an apologetic smile.

"Sorry. Forgot to mention we tend to eat lunch at our desks. Craig there goes around first thing in the morning and collects the orders," he said, pointing at the man handing out the last of the food and drinks. "But there is a cafe down on the ground floor."

Sam smiled back uncomfortably as she retrieved her purse and headed out alone, a dozen eyes following her as she went. At that moment, she was back in elementary school. Sam expected the snickering to start at any moment and felt her cheeks flush again as she left the office. Just as she rounded the corner, she heard someone call out, "Hey Jorvinski, how's babysitting going?", before someone else began to chuckle.

Once in the elevator, Sam stood silently in the back corner as people came and went on each floor they passed. None engaged her in conversation and everything continued to feel wrong. Was she really supposed to be here? The questions continued to come as she reached ground level and headed for the cafe.

Once back at her desk, things didn't get any easier, especially when an agent sitting a few feet away asked whether Sam would mind "fetching" the crew some coffees and donuts. He said being the junior agent made it her responsibility and she should try a little harder if she really wanted to fit in. None of the other agents spoke up and Sam had no choice other than to fulfill the request.

By the time she returned with a bag of donuts and 2 trays of cups, the previously filled office was completely empty. Every desk sat vacant, the silence deafening.

"Rader, why aren't you at the meeting?" a voice suddenly asked behind her. It was Houseman, the man who had welcomed her from behind his desk that morning.

"I was asked to get-"

"Just get to the meeting. Assistant Director Johnson doesn't tolerate tardiness." After setting the trays down, Sam returned to the hall and looked both ways, trying to figure out which way to go. "Rader. One floor up, left out of the elevator and 2nd door on the right."

"Thank you, Sir," she replied through gritted teeth, before heading to the elevator.

The room was filled with people to such an extent, that a dozen or more were standing around the outside of the room. The man conducting the meeting halted as she entered, then made a point of waiting until she found a place to stand. As Sam looked at the crowd, she found Jorvinski sitting near the middle, next to the man who'd asked her to get the coffees. Both wore smirks on their faces. Jorvinski pointed at his watch and shook his head, the other man laughing into his hand.

"Good to see Quantico teaching the new agents some punctuality," the presenter said, before continuing his lecture.

───────

Sam tried as hard as she could for the following week, but no matter what tactic she employed, her colleagues refused to welcome her in. She wasn't sure whether it was a sexist thing, as 3 other women worked in the office of almost 3 dozen agents. But something was refusing to give her a break.

It was as if Sam needed to somehow prove her worth to these people. Just making it through Quantico wouldn't be enough. As far as this group was concerned, agents needed to show their worth before anyone accepted them.

By the time the weekend arrived, Sam was relieved to finally enjoy a couple of days of rest. The man from the plane continued to plague her mind daily and Sam spent each evening with the business card in her hands, slowly turning it over and over.

The Friday had been particularly hard on her, with a couple of agents pranking her again, by telling her the assistant director needed her down in the foyer. Despite finding him down in the cafe having lunch with someone, he looked at her questioningly when she excused herself, interrupting his meeting. Sam was once again left red-faced when he questioned her training, saying he would let her know if he ever needed her.

It was while staring at the card that night that Sam finally made her mind up to pay the Milton Ward building a visit the following morning. That night, she slept more soundly than she'd had in a very long time. It was as if something had lifted from her shoulders and was finally giving her the space to breathe. Whatever Milton Ward had in store for her, tomorrow was the day she would find out what that was.

Sam didn't set an alarm for herself, instead opting for a sleep in. She wanted to feel as refreshed as possible, remembering how horrible the night was before her first day at work. By the time she stepped out into the warm August day the following morning, the sun was already high in a near-cloudless sky.

The Milton Ward building was on Baltimore Ave and after parking her Jeep in a nearby parking garage, Sam slowly made her way towards the entrance, looking up at the building before her. It stretched high into the sky, some 48 floors above her, the tallest building in the city. The large logo stared ominously down at her from the top floor, glinting in the morning sun.

Just before she reached the turnstile door leading into the building's foyer, Sam paused for a brief moment, looking back over her shoulder as the world continued to pass her by. None of the people walking along the sidewalk paid her any attention, the cars rolling by uninterrupted. She was a single entity on a street filled with hundreds.

The single door continued to slowly rotate, the glass reflecting her own image back at her. Sam could make out several people moving about inside the huge foyer, took a deep breath and tried to calm the nerves that had slowly built up during the brief walk from her car After a second deep breath, her feet began to move towards the door and to the uncertainty of what awaited on the other side.

The huge Milton Ward logo hung high on the wall behind the welcome desk. It looked to be made out of stainless steel, suspended in mid-air by thin cables, hung from a ceiling that appeared to stretch almost 5 floors above. Sam looked around, second guessing herself and the decision to come in the first place. It wasn't as if she had an appointment. She didn't even have a name to go along with the plain business card now grasped tightly in her pocket.

"Miss Rader?" a voice suddenly said from beside her. It was a woman, wearing a suit with the Milton Ward logo embroidered on her jacket. Sam turned to her as the beating in her chest increased.

"Yes?" she said, completely taken back.

"Could you follow me please?" The woman didn't wait for an answer, turning towards a bank of elevators along the back wall of the foyer. Sam followed, unsure of how she was recognized. Once the woman reached the elevators, she pulled back a barrier cord that was blocking one of the doors, held a security card to a small panel beside the doors, then waved Sam inside once they slowly slipped open.

"Where are we going?" Sam asked, hesitating a little.

"Don't worry. They've been expecting you." The woman smiled at her with a warmth Sam hadn't experienced since arriving in Kansas City.

"They?" she whispered cautiously, but stepped into the comfortable space before her. The elevator was quite large, mirrored on 3 sides. A soft melody played as the doors closed, then paused as a screen came to life beside her. A beating tempo began as the Milton Ward electronic advert began to play, showing people using cell phones and laptops in several locations.

"How did you know it was me?" Sam asked as they travelled up towards what she knew to be the very top of the building.

"Mr. Milton will explain everything, Ma'am," the woman replied, again reassuring Sam with the same warm smile.

"Ma'am makes me sound old," Sam said, but just as the woman nodded, the elevator began to slow, then stopped. The doors slid back to reveal a huge room before her, a glass wall looking out across the city far below. The blue sky was so bright, Sam almost instinctively reached for her sunglasses.

"Won't you take a seat? Mr. Milton won't be long."

Sam slowly stepped out from the elevator, suddenly unsure for her reasons to come. As she looked to ask her guide another question, the doors closed and she was left alone. She turned back and stepped towards the room, climbed a single stair up and found herself in what looked more like an oversized living room than an office.

There were 2 couches facing each other along one side of the space. Along another wall was a sunken area with several bean bags and large pillows scattered about that you stepped down into. There was a huge flatscreen television hanging from one wall and beside it, a painting of Milton Ward himself, the icon wearing his trademark spectacles and smile. Whomever the artist was, had captured the character of the man perfectly.

Outside of the huge floor-to-ceiling windows sat an outside sitting area, the space almost as large as the room Sam now stood in. There were several cane chairs scattered around a glass-topped table, as well as what appeared to be a small bar near the glass barrier that surrounded the rooftop decking.

A door suddenly opened somewhere behind her and Sam turned to see a man wearing a t-shirt and jeans walking towards her. His smile matched the woman who'd brought Sam up in the elevator, as warm and inviting as if they had known her all along.

"Miss Rader, so good to finally meet you. I'm John Milton." Sam stepped towards him, held her hand out to meet his then paused. John Milton?

The pair shook, his hand feeling warm to the touch and he gave Sam's hand a reassuring squeeze.

"Everything OK?" he asked, gesturing for Sam to take a seat.

"Yes, it's just that I was expecting..." she began, dropping onto one of the couches.

"Milton Ward?" John said, sitting opposite her. "Xavier will be along shortly. He's just held up on a call. Would you care for a hot drink?" Another man suddenly appeared, seemingly out of nowhere. He held a tray in one hand and as he neared Sam, lowered it to reveal 3 cups, the one closest to her holding black coffee. "Black with one sugar, right?"

Sam nodded, took the cup and began to feel a little like Alice in Wonderland. John Milton took one of the other cups, then waited as the man set the final cup down on the table and disappeared back through the other door.

"How did you know?" Sam said, holding her cup up slightly.

"Forgive us, but we make it our business to know everything about possible recruits. We have to when in our line of business. No good having something sudden spring up at an inappropriate time."

"Cell phones?" Sam asked, feeling more confused than before she entered the building. John Milton began to laugh at that, but it wasn't condescending. The sound was more jovial than that.

"I'm sorry, I hope John isn't making fun of you," another voice suddenly said and Sam turned to see a much older man walking towards them. John stood as the second man approached.

"Sam, this is Xavier Ward." Sam stood and shook with the man, feeling more confused than ever.

"Pleased to meet you," she said, hoping to sound as such.

"You see? I told you we'd just confuse the poor girl," Xavier Ward said as he sat and reached for his coffee.

"I'm sorry, it's just that I always thought-" she began, but John cut her off.

"Milton Ward is just a figurehead, so to speak. Someone to go out and face the public, do the appearances, sit through the interviews. You know, the boring stuff. It gives Xavier and I the chance to get on with the important stuff. Like the reason for you to come and visit with us today."

"Milton Ward isn't real?" Sam asked, sipping her coffee as if to hide behind the cup.

"Well, he's real, just not the person people think he is," Xavier said. He stood, looked at the painting of the company's figurehead and began to stroll as he spoke.

"John and I weren't brought together by cell phones or laptops, or any other type of consumer product we develop. The commercial side of our business helps us to finance the real purpose behind our brand. Do you know what the word "Pogrom" means?"

"Yes. It means violent massacre, usually against a group of people. I think the Nazis used it against the Jews, didn't they?"

"I told you she would be perfect," Xavier said to John before continuing. "Yes, it is. It could also mean a final solution against a group of people. Well, my dear, we are a final solution against a particular group of people. Why don't I let John tell the next part? He's always better at this bit. I get too emotional." Xavier sat as John took a sip from his cup, stood and took the floor from his partner.

"Sam, Xavier and I didn't come together through work, or business ventures or anything like that. We were brought together by tragedy. Each of us suffered terribly because of certain events and it was those that eventually led us to combine our grief and build a way for us to overcome it. Not just overcome it, but make sure we would save others from facing the same pain we did."

He paused, looked out through the windows and pondered his next words. Sam took a sip, then held the cup in her lap, finding herself deeply intrigued.

"Fifteen years ago, my son was murdered by a man called James Bolton. Does the name ring a bell?" Sam recognized the name instantly. "He was a serial killer that killed twelve people in California. Around the same time my boy was taken, Xavier's daughter was killed by another serial killer. Eric Tully was a serial killer working his way through central America, his victims numbering eight. Faucett isn't a place Xavier holds close."

He paused, Sam understanding the man struggling with a grief that would never diminish. Once back under control, he turned back to her and continued.

"I struggled with my emotions for a long time. Jasper's mom had died a couple of years prior to his death and once he was taken from me, there seemed little point to continuing. After spending more than a few nights at the bottom of a whiskey bottle, I was finally convinced to seek help. I found that help by way of a support group for grieving parents. It was where I met Xavier and I'm thankful I did, because once we understood each other, I knew I had found my new purpose in life."

"It didn't take us long to know what we needed to do," Xavier said, retaking the floor. "We were both already quite wealthy from our various business ventures. But once we pooled our resources, we both knew we'd be unstoppable. It was John that first floated the idea of Milton Ward. And I must say, that once it took hold, grew far beyond anything I could have imagined. It gave us resources, control, power, finances and the means to grow what we needed to make things happen."

"To make what happen?" Sam asked.

"To catch the killers, of course," John offered.

"Not just catch them, my dear. End them. Do you know where James Bolton is at this very moment? Enjoying the fresh air and sunshine of some Florida prison. And Eric Tully? Probably the same. They didn't pay for their crimes. Their lawyers got them off, pleaded them down to a life sentence instead of the death sentence they deserved."

"We have our own investigators, Sam. Our own agents, you might say. They go deep under cover to locate serial killers and only when they are a hundred percent certain, do they take action. We are the final solution to those serial killers. We began a pogrom against the evil that hides beneath the shadows of this country." John sat down again and drank his coffee.

"And there's one particularly brutal kind of killer that is dominant above all others. The cannibal. Do you know what a cannibal is, Sam?"

"Yes, someone that eat's the flesh of another person."

"Yes, and no.," Xavier said, shaking his head a little. "Cannibals are to reality, as what vampires are to myth. Cannibals not only eat the flesh of their victims, they *crave* it, just like a vampire craves blood. These cannibals gain strength with each victim. Have you ever heard of the name Harry Lightman?"

Sam's cheeks began to heat up at hearing the name. She lifted the cup to her lips to try and hide the blush from the two men, but they didn't wait for an answer, John picking up the story.

"Harry Lightman was your great grandfather, a monster that murdered a lot of people. But he was also a cannibal.

There's one thing we know for sure. These cannibals some-times pass on their hunger to their offspring." The burning continued to rise in Sam's face. "Please don't be embarrassed. We know you're not a psychotic killer."

"But we do know that you have the same urges as your great grandfather. We also know your mother had them before she died. Do you remember Tim?' John stood and Sam was surprised to see another man standing beside him, one she recognized instantly. It was the man from the plane.

Before she had a chance to stand, the newcomer held his hand out, shook hers and sat on the couch opposite.

"In 1979, Jeffrey Dahmer fathered an illegitimate child with a woman called Amanda Kitchener. Tim here, is that child." Xavier's words hung in the air for a brief moment, Sam finding the information almost shocking to hear.

"It's true," Tim said, nodding as he smiled at her. "But don't worry, I won't try and take a bite." John chuckled a little and sat beside Sam.

"Wasn't Dahmer a homosexual?" Sam asked. John stepped forward to answer.

"Yes, for most of his life. But he was also a heavy drinker and when he was nineteen years old, he spent a single moment with a woman who took advantage of a severely intoxicated kid, fell pregnant and subsequently had a son." Xavier continued.

"We have fourteen agents, if that's what you want to call them. They all work in pairs and hunt the dozens of active serial killers currently haunting this great country of ours. But we don't arrest them. We are the reason some of these so called "killing streaks" seem to end for no reason. If you decide to join us, Sam, then you get to fulfill that craving that has been lurking inside you all these years. If you manage to find one of these monsters, you end them, any way you choose. No cops, no trial, and no fucking lawyers. Do you understand?"

The three of them now sat opposite her and watched with

intrigue. They had laid it all out on the line and were waiting to see if Sam would accept.

She sat uncomfortably before them, a little unsure of what she was supposed to say. The fact Dahmer's son was now sitting across from her, didn't make the situation any easier. It was Xavier that sat forward and broke the silence.

"Why don't we take this outside?" he said, pointing out through the windows.

If Milton Ward did anything well, it was looking after guests. Within seconds of the four of them taking their seats outside, an entire catering crew began to assemble all manner of foods before them. It was like a smorgasbord of delights, from which each of the party began to assemble their own plate of food.

Sam was still feeling very overwhelmed as she began to nibble on a decadent fruit salad, but the distraction of food helped a lot. It seemed to take the focus off her for the moment, the two billionaires briefly discussing a different matter entirely. Tim sat opposite her, chomping down on a slice of garlic bread. He kept stealing glances at the woman sitting across, himself more than a little nervous.

"I wasn't sure whether you'd come," he finally said.

"Neither was I, but you were right."

"About what?" he asked.

"About not fitting in down there. They really don't make it easy, do they? How did you know?" Sam popped a piece of watermelon into her mouth, the coolness tasting refreshing.

"Been there myself."

"Wait. You were with the FBI?" She didn't know why the news surprised her, but it did.

"Yah, four years. The very outfit you were assigned to, in fact. I remember my first day, stepping into that huge office and having all the agents stare at me. Then that asshole giving me the whole welcome speech. How is Watson?"

Sam thought back to the beast of a man that sat behind his desk as he welcomed her. It wasn't the reception she'd anticipated, despite her own tardiness.

"On fire when I saw him last," she quipped.

"Anyone welcome you with open arms?"

"Ah no, not one." And that was when Tim said something that took Sam completely by surprise.

"It took me a long time to understand the cravings I was feeling. A *very* long time." She looked at him, a grape half way to her mouth.

"I-" she began, but wasn't sure what she wanted to ask.

"I'm sorry. Crap just seems to come out of my mouth willy-nilly. I didn't mean to embarrass you." Sam did feel a slight flush warm her cheeks, but she fought it back.

"No, please. It's just that I've never discussed it with anyone before. My mom died when I was still quite young. I only read her suicide note a few days ago."

"I'm sorry about your mom. She must have done it tough, not talking to anyone about it."

"I can't imagine what it was like for her. But she did have my dad."

"Ah yes, Samuel." Sam looked at him curiously. "Oh, yes. I'm sorry. I did do my research on you before the day on the plane. Had to be sure you would be suitable for this position." He smiled at her as he popped a strawberry into his mouth.

"Oh, yeah? What else did you find out?"

After spending time in intimate chats while eating, the table was finally cleared and the four of them were once again alone. The sun shone brightly above them and as the heat of the day continued to bite into them, Xavier pulled out a remote control from his pocket and pointed it at the windows behind them.

A whirring sound, coming from somewhere behind the walls, filled the air. To Sam's surprise, an awning began to slide out from a groove in the wall and slowly fed itself across the rooftop a few feet above their heads. It was made from some sort of clear material, but as the buzzing came to a halt, the material darkened until it blocked out the sun completely.

"Neat trick, huh?" Tim said, smiling at Sam.

Xavier pocketed the remote and turned back to the group. His friendly demeanor disappeared like the midday sun and his tone took a turn Sam immediately understood.

"So, what do you think of our little proposal? Think you have what it takes?"

3

Sam was thankful for the opportunity and even more so when both Xavier and John gave her time to think. As Sam made the journey back to her car, she felt overwhelmed by the generosity of the people she met, but also incredibly torn. The confusion stemmed from the group understanding her inner battles more than she. Particularly the strange thoughts she had whenever she watched a murder on television.

Given the complexity of her constant emotional battle, Sam at first felt under-qualified for what the group asked of her. But just as she neared the corner, a voice suddenly shouted out to her.

"Samantha, one sec." She turned to see Tim running towards her. He slowed when he saw her turn. Once close enough, he paused to catch his breath. "Would you mind taking a drive with me?"

After a few turns, Tim took them onto Highway 169 and began

to head north out of the city. He made a little small talk, but once he switched the cruise control on, changed the direction of the conversation.

"I totally understand your hesitation," he began. "The best way I can describe it is like someone finding out about a bad habit you've tried to hide your whole life." He looked at her briefly, then turned his eyes back to the road. "Those weird feelings, they don't seem to make sense and you spend years trying to figure them out. I didn't find out who my father was until I was almost 20 years old."

"That must have been tough," Sam said. Tim paused, pondered and slowly nodded.

"Yah, tough it was. But I didn't let it beat me. Instead, I used the help John and Xavier offered and began to understand it. It's not easy learning you come from a cannibal background. But it's a trait that's in all of us. Think about it. One of our core instincts is survival, regardless of the consequences. There was a plane crash in the Andes Mountains back in '72. A football team and their families. They were stuck so high in the mountains that no-one was going to find them. Know what happened once the hunger pains became too bad?"

But Sam had heard this story herself and already knew of the gruesome reality from that flight and the eventual discovery.

"Yah, I know that one."

"It comes from ancient times. Cannibalism is part of nature. There are tons of animals in the wild that eat their young. In the oceans, on the plains, in the air, it's everywhere. We aren't that far from that wilderness we came from." Sam knew what he meant, but felt apprehensive to discuss it.

"Where are you taking me?" she asked, subtly trying to change the direction of the conversation. Tim looked at her briefly before answering. He understood her apprehension better than anyone, so understood that giving her time would be the best course of action.

"Somewhere where we make a difference."

Thirty minutes later, Tim turned his truck onto State Route 92 and headed west. The fields passed them by as their conversation faded out. Sam felt her head fill with all sorts of thoughts, some of which were memories from her past, memories that only now began to make sense.

After another 10 minutes or so, the truck began to slow, before turning onto a small gravel road. It led up towards a large gate and once the truck neared it, it swung slowly open for them.

"Here we are," Time whispered, slightly waving a finger at a camera that sat on one of the gate's pillars.

"What is this place?"

"This is where the magic happens," Tim replied.

They continued on for a couple of minutes. The small driveway continued up and around the side of a hill where a small farm building stood. It looked like a quaint little cottage and there was an elderly woman sitting on the veranda, her rocking chair slowly swinging back and forth as her knitting needles danced in her hands.

Once Tim pulled the truck up, they climbed out and Sam stretched her legs.

"Hi Agnes," Tim called to the old woman and she waved back with a smile. "This here is a real working farm. Agnes there has been the caretaker of the property for over 20 years." He stopped, looked out across the valley below and found what he was looking for. "See that dust cloud down there?" Sam nodded. "That's Frank, Agnes's husband."

There were 2 sheds opposite the cottage. One had a small

chimney on its side, while the other had a small aerial on the roof. Once inside, there was a single door and when opened, it revealed a small foyer with a second door.

Tim held a security card to an undefined spot on the wall beside the door, smiling at her as he did.

"Ready for the rabbit hole, Alice?" he quipped, before the second door slid aside to reveal an elevator. "After you." Tim gestured for Sam to enter, then followed her. Inside, there were 3 rows of buttons on the touch panel beside the door. But they all appeared beneath 2 other buttons that sat in a row above the middle column.

"Weird," Sam whispered.

"Not really. See, once you get down 2 floors, the elevator also travels sideways." He pressed a button marked "D", stepped back and watched as the door quietly slid shut. "John and Xavier built this compound over the course of a few years. Now it goes down six floors and 3 rooms wide. It's pretty cool. There's a kind of grid track facing the rooms and it travels along those tracks. There are actually two elevators and they move completely independently."

Sam watched a small panel above the door where it displayed a grid pattern, the flashing dot traveling down the center. She felt herself slow, then brace as her balance shifted left.

"Takes a bit of getting used to," Tim said. The door slid open to reveal a large room that instantly reminded Sam of the main office back at the FBI building. There was a row of desks along one wall and dozens of monitors on the other. Each of the screens was hooked up to a camera, although the images made little sense to her.

"What is this?" she whispered, stepping from the elevator. The half a dozen people sitting at a couple of the desks looked up, smiled and waved. Two of them stood and walked towards her.

"Sam, welcome," one said, holding his hand out to her. "I'm Bert. This is Clare." He pointed at the woman following him. Sam shook with each of them, then followed it up when the others also approached.

"This is what you'd call the central hub of our little operation. Those monitors tune in on known suspects, possible victims, possible future suspects and so on."

"Possible future suspects?" she asked.

"Yes, the software analyses all known relatives, traits, upbringing and other factors, then spits out the likelihood that that person may turn nasty," Clare said. She pointed to a number of computer terminals on the far wall. "Those are the input stations. They link directly to a number of federal databases we have access to. It's a pretty broad setup and gives us information in real time." Sam felt herself impressed.

"Is that legal?" she wondered out loud.

"Both John and Xavier have quite a few connections that reach all the way to the White House. This," he began, waving a hand around the office, "is one way to avoid bureaucratic red tape."

"But how can you…" she began, but Tim held a hand up.

"I'm sure you have a thousand questions. I promise to answer all of them, but first, let me show you what I came here for." He turned to the others. "Thanks, guys." They nodded, smiled a final time at Sam, then returned to their previous seats.

"This place isn't what you might think," Tim began once the elevator door closed. "It's so much more than that." He pressed a button with what looked like a smiley face, then stepped back.

Sam had a million questions rushing around her head, but she tried to keep them held back for the time being. It was pointless asking them before seeing the entire picture and somehow, knew the following destination would come close to answering most of them.

The flashing dot on the display showed the elevator first dropping to the bottom-most level, then over to the far left. When the door opened, the room that came into view was dark and somber-looking.

There was some kind of gentle background music playing, the kind meant to relax. A small room sat between the elevator door and an open archway and Sam could see something highlighted on the wall of the large room she was about to enter.

The entire room looked like a giant dome, the walls reaching from a central meeting point, down towards the floor in a smooth arc. In the very center of the room stood a crystal column with a rounded top. It looked like a giant lollipop, but inside the crystal ball was a single word, one that could be read from wherever a person stood: Justice.

Around the dome's outer wall, looking as if painted on, were rows of bright stars that stretched from the ceiling down towards the floor. Each line differed in length, with some only four or five stars long, while others had dozens. But at the base of each line, as if birthing each row of stars upwards, was a red light with a skull on it.

As Sam stood and stared curiously at the strange room before her, a star suddenly bloomed at the end of a row close to her. It was then she saw that it was a kind of holographic projection. There were dozens of rows of these stars, most tied to the red skulls. Those rows that didn't have the skulls, instead had 2 words floating beneath them: Be Free.

"What is this place?" Sam asked, watching as another star bloomed on the wall across from her. She turned to look at Tim as he sat on a stoop near the crystal column. His face was illuminated enough for Sam to see he was crying. "Tim?"

"This is what it's for, Sam." She didn't follow.

"What is?"

"Each of those rows signifies a string of victims. They are where we have identified a serial killer at work. Those with the red skulls indicate an active killer. The ones we have ended have been replaced with those words, essentially freeing them from their nightmares."

Sam turned back to look at the lights, now understanding the scope of the nightmares the room represented. There must have been hundreds of stars, each one a victim. She counted thirty-two red skulls around the base of the dome.

"That many?" she almost whispered.

"More. We just haven't found them yet." He stood and walked to her. "This is what we end, Samantha. We stop the killing, the suffering, the anguish. We don't end them until we are 100% sure of their guilt, normally by catching them in the act. There can be no second guessing with this. We are the reason so many killing sprees suddenly end. Many might believe that the killer may have died, or been imprisoned, or stopped of their own accord, but we know better. Because we are the reason for it. And these are only from the past couple of years. Want to see the actual numbers?"

Sam nodded, although unsure of what he meant. She watched as he touched the crystal ball near the base, pushing a button of some kind. Stars began to blink on around the dome, sometimes three or four at a time. Whole strings blinked into life, until the whole room was almost completely illuminated, bathed in what could have been daylight.

With her mouth open, Sam looked around the room, the lights overlapping in places. Around the base were dozens of skulls, some red, some white.

"How many?" she asked.

"122 serials killers so far. The hundreds of victims you see lit up here could have been thousands if we hadn't stopped them. This," he said, pointing at all the sparkling stars, "all this, is about the lives we saved."

Feeling overwhelmed with surprise, Sam knelt down, staring at the lit-up wall around her, each light signifying a victim; someone's child, someone's partner; someone's lover. So many people taken before their time.

It was more than overwhelming to understand the significance of the memorial room. What this organization had done, was not only save thousands of man hours on a system already struggling, not only save hundreds of thousands of dollars of tax payer money housing the perpetrators for decades to come, but more importantly, it had saved countless lives of innocent people.

"I don't know what to say," Sam said, still looking at all the lights, some fading out again.

"Say yes," Tim whispered back at her. "Say you'll join us and help. You have exactly what we need."

As Tim spoke, Sam suddenly saw an odd string of stars behind him. The light sprouting the string wasn't red or white, but a faint green. And neither a skull, nor the words "Be Free" were there, instead the word "Saved". The green light had 2 faint stars above it, but just as she saw them, they began to fade.

"What's-" but as she began to ask, they were gone and Tim was still talking about her joining.

"We've had our eye on you for a long time, Sam. The connections that feed us information from Quantico put you in the highest bracket of suitability for us. Your background, your intelligence, your demeanor, your heritage, your skills; they all come together in this place. This is where you belong."

Sam stood and walked closer to him, more to see whether the strange green light had in fact gone. When she couldn't find it amongst the remaining lights, Sam decided to let it go for the time being, instead addressing his question.

"It's probably not the answer you're looking for right now, but do you think I could have a day to think about it? It's just that it has been a lot of information to take in. I worked so hard to get to where I am and I didn't consider running away from it a week in, just because of a few unwelcoming people."

Despite looking a little rejected, Tim slowly nodded his head. Although he had a vastly different introduction to the team, he understood how hard it must have been for her.

"Of course, I understand." His face suddenly brightened and he clicked his fingers as if an idea suddenly sparked in his brain. "Hey, you haven't met momma."

After walking back into the elevator, Tim pressed the button right in the middle of the panel marked with a C. Sam felt the strange sensation of the car taking her across the grid, then upwards. When the doors slid open, there was a small office-like room with another wall of monitors facing the only desk. Sitting at the desk was a woman that can only be described as a walking rainbow.

She stood the second the elevator doors opened, her warm smile filling Sam with warmth before she'd even introduced herself.

"Child, you're here. I'm Madeline Jackson. But you can call me momma. Everyone else does." Sam held out her hand, but the woman pulled her in and gave her a hug that left Samantha reeling for air.

"Pleased to meet you. I'm Sam."

"I know you are. Has Tim here given you the tour yet?"

"Most of it, yes. Just came from the memorial room." Momma's face turned solemn.

"Certainly is an eye opener." She waved an arm around her room. "Well, this is me," she said, eyeing Sam off.

"What do you do here?"

"Momma is what you might call the central nervous system of Pogrom. Without her, we wouldn't get very far at all," Tim said. momma chortled an embarrassed laugh.

"I'm sure you kids would do just well without me." Turning to Sam, she said, "Come, I'll show you."

She took Sam by the arm and led her back to the desk. There were several screens on her desk, working in conjunction with the monitors hanging on the wall. It looked like most of the monitors had live feeds from security cameras. Others had news reports running, but the volume was silenced.

"This is where I try and find those we suspect of wrongdoing. In my past life I was a criminal investigative analyst for the FBI in Chicago. But John Milton recruited me several years ago and well? Here I am."

"You were a profiler with the FBI?" momma looked at her a little surprised, but with a glint of warmth in her eye.

"That surprises you?" Sam felt her cheeks warm a little, a habit she loathed at the best of times.

"No, that's not what I meant," she said quickly. "I only meant that-" momma began to chuckle a little at that.

"I know what you meant, child. Come. Take a seat and check out what I can help you with."

Sam sat at the desk and watched as momma moved a few folders aside, then reached for what looked like a secondary keyboard. Only this keyboard had a whole lot of numbers instead of letters. She fiddled with a couple of them, then punched the enter key.

The bank of monitors on the wall turned into a single screen as a map of the United States appeared, each state highlighted with a couple of cities here and there. Kansas City was one of them, as were Washington, Chicago, Los Angeles, Houston, Richmond and many more.

"These are all the active cases we have right now. Our system has access to more than a thousand databases around the country and this gives us a complete picture of every single death in the country in real time. Each one is analyzed, scrutinized and tenderized until we are positive it isn't related to any known homicide track we're working on. Those we consider related, well they get shifted into our 'further investigation required' pile. Here." momma punched another button and the map changed into a single state on the left and a vast list of names on the right. There were dozens of names, each linked to a specific city in the shown state.

The states began to slowly cycle, first California, then Missouri, Arizona, Texas, Missouri. When Sam saw Kansas City, she appeared surprised.

"There's a serial killer in Kansas City?" momma paused the screen.

"Aha."

"But I haven't heard anything on the news."

"That's because they don't know," Tim offered from beside her. Sam looked at him with surprise.

"He's right," momma added. "This killer has been active for going on 7 years now. 8 victims, all died from knife wounds and all spread across the city. The police and the media simply put each down as robberies gone wrong." momma looked at Tim and gave him a nudge. "But we know better, don't we?"

"We certainly do."

"How?" Sam asked.

"May I?" momma asked and Sam stood, returning the desk to its handler. momma sat, reached for the primary keyboard and began to type like a mini whirlwind. Within seconds, several photos appeared on the giant screen before them.

Each photo showed a dead body lying on a medical table.

Beside the first photo was a second photo of the crime scene where the person died. Each one had died in a home, the victim normally found dead in bed. Out of all the photos, one was found in the bathroom, while another in the kitchen.

Sam looked at each picture and tried to see the similarity of which momma and Tim spoke of. But after a minute or 2, was unable to find the connection.

"I don't see it," she finally said.

"That's because you don't know about this," momma offered and punched a couple of buttons. A new photo appeared beside the others, showing happy people with their pet dogs.

"Their pets?" Sam asked.

"Correct. In every case the dogs went missing, never to be found again," Tim whispered beside her ear. "The K9 Killer."

"You call him-" Sam began, but momma cut her off.

"No, that's not what we call the person responsible."

"That's what *I* call him," Tim said sheepishly.

"Every dog missing? They all had dogs?" Sam continued.

"Every one of them," momma said. Sam took a step towards the screens, eyeing each of the images intently. She pointed to one and then another.

"Couldn't they have just run away? It looks like the front doors could have been opened. Maybe?"

"A few even had doggy doors, if you want to get right down to it. But the thing is, according the victim's families, none of the dogs were ever found again. Given the time between killings and the distances between them, no one has really been able to link any of them. 5 of the murders have been in and around the city, but we're talking a single murder amongst almost a hundred which occurred some years. And each is always in a different area, 4 in outlying towns."

"But how do you know they're linked?" Sam asked. She watched momma give Tim an uncomfortable look, the pair appearing to connect with each other telepathically. When he gave a brief nod, momma pressed a single button.

"Because of these."

The screen went blank for a split second, before 8 images appeared in a grid. The gruesome nature of the photos took only a second to comprehend and Sam saw the link almost instantly. Each image showed a tree with something hanging suspended from a branch by a rope. It reminded Sam of lynchings she'd seen in several movies.

Tied by their back legs were dogs, each hanging like a slaughtered animal in an abattoir killing room. Their breed could only be determined by the color and nature of their coats, as their heads had been completely pulverized by whatever blunt object had been used to smash them in. The pool of blood beneath them suggested the animal died where it hung.

Sam held a hand up to her mouth, horrified by the images. The link between each scene was clear with the nature of the injuries to each animal, as well as how they were left hanging. The images suddenly blinked out, replaced by a map of Kansas City and the outlying areas. momma zoomed out even more, until 4 states were in view, 8 dots scattered between them.

"Those animals have been found in those areas. Nebraska, Iowa, Kansas and Missouri. Given the areas where they were found, none of the agencies would have linked the deaths over such a time period. Whoever this is, understands that time and distance is giving them the edge. But *we* know about them."

momma snapped a button and the screen returned to its previous state, each monitor displaying a different picture.

"That killer has been dormant for 7 months now. We expect a new killing any day now. But," she waved at the screens, "that's just one amongst many. Think I'd better get back to work." She smiled at Sam, who forced one in return.

"I do have one question, if I may," Sam said, suddenly remembering the Memorial Room. "When we were in the memorial room, there was one string of stars that had a green base. What was that for?"

momma froze, as did Tim. The pair looked at each other for a moment, again as if linked telepathically. Sam wondered whether she had asked a wrong question, when Tim answered.

"Maybe leave that story for another day. Thanks, momma," he said, turning to her and giving momma a hug. She returned it, then gave Sam one as well.

"We could use your help, Samantha. There's work to be done and it's the kind of work you could really sink your teeth into." She winked at Sam then sat back at her desk.

Tim was already by the elevator door and when it slid shut a moment later, momma turned to her a final time and winked.

10 minutes later, Tim turned the truck back onto the main road and flicked on the cruise control. Sam watched the landscape pass by with her head filled with thoughts.

"I know how confusing you must feel right now. But I promise that a week in, you'll feel like you've been part of the team for years."

"That last thing momma said to me. Does she really think I'm cannibalistic?" Tim looked at her.

"No. But she knows that the cravings live inside you, just like they do me." He paused, looked through his driver's side window and took a deep breath.

"What is it?" Sam asked. He didn't answer for a long time, simply holding the wheel steady, the knuckles turning white from the effort he put into his grip. "Tim?"

"The cravings live inside everybody. I spoke to a professor at a university during a nearby investigation and he gave me a whole spiel about how we evolved from beings that would do anything for the sake of survival. It's just that..." He paused again.

"Go on," Sam offered empathically. He looked at her again, his feelings of sharing the information unnerving him some. After a minute, Tim began his own tale.

4

S am listened as the countryside drifted past them. Tim began slowly at first, a revelation she wasn't expecting.

"I was 12 years old when I first joined Pogrom. It was John that recruited me, in fact."

"Wait, what? 12?" Sam asked, completely surprised.

"That green light in the memorial room?" He paused again, the anguish clear on his face, then swallowed a deep breath before continuing. "That green light is me." Sam felt goosebumps prickle her arms as he spoke, unable to contain her shock.

"What?" she whispered.

"It's true. The green light is me and the 2 stars above? Those are my mom and sister." His voice wavered a bit and Sam suddenly felt guilty at prying into his business.

"Please," she said, reaching out and touching his arm. "You don't have to."

"No, seriously. It's OK." He paused yet again, then reached for a packet of cigarettes and lit one. Once he'd drawn on it a couple of times, he continued. "I killed them. It was before anyone had told me who my father really was. But I remember the haunting visions, the weird thoughts that ran through my head every waking hour. My fascination with dead animals, and live ones that I murdered." He looked at Sam. "Did you ever have those thoughts run through your head?"

She thought back to the rabbit laying on that long-ago track and to her own pet cemetery. She thought back to the confrontation at school, the taste of the blood and the way the warmth of it had made her feel complete in a way.

"Yes, I understand those feelings." Her words barely registered, but Tim heard them just the same.

"I killed my mother first. She was a drunk and often molested me after I'd gone to bed. That particular night was the first time she ever brought me to..." he paused again. His cheeks looked flushed and Sam could tell it wasn't easy. She tried again to stop him.

"Honestly, you don't have to."

"It was the first time I had ever, you know, "gone". She began to laugh at me, that drunken stink-filled torment of a laugh filled my bedroom. She laid back on the pillow beside me; called me a "princess" and closed her eyes. I remember just lying there for a moment, the heat of the liquid still hot on my leg, my penis itching like mad. And there she was, lying next to me and laughing. I leant over, kissed her forehead and whispered goodbye. She had just enough time to open her eyes before I lunged at her throat and began to bite. She fought me, but how strong do you think a drunk woman is, especially one who weighed only slightly more than the pillow she rested her head on?"

Sam watched as he drew on his cigarette, blew the smoke from his nose and stared at the road ahead.

"It didn't take long for her struggles to ebb away. Her blood filled the bed around us and once I finished, the taste of blood really hit me for the first time. As I walked from her room towards the bathroom, my sister arrived home. She was 19 and had been out with her boyfriend. He'd offered me drugs a few times and I knew he'd given them to her. Anyway, she didn't see me hiding in one of the doorways and just went to her own room. It was at the other end of the house and she wasn't one for small talk. Whenever she was home, she would lock herself into her room and only come out for bathroom and food breaks."

A loud engine suddenly roared beside them and Sam looked to see a Harley Davidson pass them at speed.

"Idiot," she muttered.

"Anyway, I waited until I didn't hear any noises from her room and then slipped in and killed her the same way. But there was something that happened with her that hadn't with my mom." Tim looked curiously at Sam, as if asking her for the answer.

"What?"

"I enjoyed it. The taste; the sensation of her flesh in my mouth; the warmth. It was as if I was scratching an itch that had lived inside me for years." Sam remembered the taste of the flesh from her own childhood nightmare. " I don't know whether you understand-"

"I do, honest. I...had my own experience in a roundabout way. I totally understand."

"The next morning, I panicked and ran. The bodies were found the following day and I was picked up in Arizona 2 weeks later. The cops brought me back to Milwaukee and it was there that John Milton found me. I guess the rest is history."

Sam watched as Tim stubbed his cigarette out, a single tear rolling down his cheek. She gave his arm a squeeze and sat back.

"I can't imagine what that must have been like."

"The man is like the father I should have had. It was he who put me through school and offered me anything I wanted. Of course, I chose the FBI, at that stage not knowing about the true nature of Pogrom. But, eventually, I found that there was a much higher purpose for me and now, here I am."

The traffic began to build as the truck reached the outskirts of the city. Sam thought about all that had happened and wondered whether she should accept. But something inside her refused to give in, instead willing her to wait.

"Tim, I'm sorry, but I need to sleep on it. I understand everything you guys do, but I really worked my ass off to get to where I am. I can't just throw it away."

"We don't force anyone. Of course, you can take your time, but please, keep what you've seen to yourself. Otherwise, you know, I'll have to kill you."

Samantha climbed into her car with a new sense of confusion in her mind. The confusion wasn't about what she had seen, but rather about the decision that needed to be made. The decision would see her abandon a dream she'd carried for more than half her life, a dream her father had helped to make a reality with vigorous training, both mental and physical.

Even her mother had given Sam a sense of what she wanted to do with her life, despite not being around for the majority of it. It was the experiences and anxiety Judith had gone through for so long that gave Sam part of the determination to help bring change to people's lives.

During the drive back to her apartment, Sam remembered her father's guidance through the years, particularly the training he'd bestowed on her. Living up in the mountain and away from the prying eyes of the townsfolk had given them both the space needed to get Sam's emotions and instincts under control.

As she made her way through traffic, Sam recalled herself struggling with similar "cravings" that Tim had divulged. But she had never thought of them as being cannibalistic before. In her mind, she put them down as being the murderous instincts of a serial killer, her great grandfather maybe passing on some of his own to her.

Harry Lightman had been a prolific killer, one of Australia's worst for many decades. There was a very good chance that his murderous ways could have made their way to her, but cannibalistic? That was a term that hadn't crossed her mind.

Reading her mother's letter had brought a lot of emotions back for her and Sam felt the overwhelming words intertwining with that day's revelations. Milton Ward had been revealed to her like a stolen item being sold from the back of a truck. It was information she needed to keep concealed and yet, her first instinct was to phone home and tell her father. To have him help her put everything where it should be.

Samuel Rader had always found ways to keep his daughter focused, no matter how bad the situation. Raising her single-handedly after Judith's passing mustn't have been easy, especially when raising a psychotic daughter with a serial-killer demeanor. But he'd succeeded where so many would have failed.

Sam looked across at the car next to her while waiting for the traffic light to turn green. A man and a woman sat in the front seats of an SUV, arguing about something. She thought back to Bobby, a man she'd met at Quantico the first day of her training. The couple sitting beside her in traffic reminded her so much of the constant arguing her own brief relationship with Bobby had turned into. The endless niggling and silly fights.

A car honked behind Sam and she saw the light had turned green before her.

"Sorry," she called into the rearview mirror, waving her hand before taking off. She just wanted to get home, take off her clothes and climb into a hot bath. Sam believed them to be one of life's true luxuries; an experience to be savored and left for times of need. A bubble bath had the power to heal many issues, the least of which was confusion and anxiety, and today, she felt them both.

The underground carpark of her apartment building was more abandoned than usual when Sam finally pulled into her space a short while later. There was a crashing and banging coming from one of the far corners and she could see Mr. Paddington emptying one of the garbage trolleys from under one of the chutes. He waved when he spotted Sam.

She returned his wave and punched the elevator button, now keener to get home than ever. The tub was already calling her and she could feel the anxiety building the closer she got to her front door. The doors finally slid open as Mr. Paddington began to wheel the trolley back to its place. Sam pushed the number 8 button and stood back as the doors closed.

The elevator rattled a little as it climbed and Sam thought back to the curious experience of a sideways elevator she'd travelled in that very day. But she snapped the thought away, instead wanting to concentrate on the task at hand; to get to her apartment and lose the day's concerns.

The elevator dinged, slowed, then stopped, opening its doors to reveal the foyer of the 8th floor. 2 elevators served the building, each sitting on opposite walls. There was a man facing the other one, a large canvas bag sitting by his feet. He had the hood of his jumper pulled over his head and didn't turn as Sam stepped out. The doors before him slid open and he lifted the bag inside. Sam briefly watched him, but when he didn't turn to push the button, she headed to her door.

It was less than 5 minutes later that Sam finally stepped into the bath, the heat feeling insanely welcoming as she lowered herself into the water. She'd run it hotter than usual, hoping for the higher temperature to rip the worries of the day from her mind. As she laid back, the magic began to work immediately, like a warm hug. Once Sam closed her eyes and let the waters do their thing, she felt all the anxiety of the day melt away.

———

It wasn't often that Sam fell asleep in the bath, but this time she did, waking to water that was already cold enough to chill her body. She was shaking uncontrollably as she stood and rather than refilling the bath, decided to jump into the shower for a quick reheat.

Once she felt her core temperature rise above frigid, Sam hopped back out, wrapped herself up in 2 large towels and headed for the kitchen. With the day's worries all but gone for the moment and her temperature back to normal, the next thing she needed to take care of were the hunger pains now grumbling somewhere inside her middle. And there was only one thing that ever fixed these particular type of hunger pains: pancakes.

Sam began to assemble the ingredients for her snack, remembering that she had the buttermilk her father always added to the batter. It was the quintessential additive that gave his pancakes the yummy twist she enjoyed.

But when she looked in the fridge, Sam found another key ingredient missing, remembering that she'd used the last of the eggs that very morning. Without at least a single egg, the pancake batter wouldn't work. She knew, having attempted the very thing a few years prior. The resultant glug did not resemble anything worthy of being named pancakes, ending up in the trash.

Sam considered heading out to the store, but after debating about it, decided not to. It wasn't worth the effort. She could make something else, but her taste buds had made up their mind. As she reconsidered the store, Sam suddenly remembered Kathleen, the neighbor she'd briefly met the previous morning. Maybe *she* could spare a couple of eggs until Sam could return them. Considering her cravings, Sam decided that a trip next door would be perfect and after donning a dressing gown, headed out.

The hallway was deserted and she quickly made her way to her neighbor's door. As she reached up to knock, Sam's stomach instantly knotted as she saw the door standing slightly ajar. It wasn't open enough to notice if you weren't looking, but standing before it with her hand up and ready to wrap on it, the gap was more than evident.

"Maybe she just forgot to shut it," Sam told herself, but that was when she looked down to the floor. There was a small red splotch on the tiles. With her heart quickening, Sam knelt down and slowly touched a finger to the congealed goo. It smeared and Sam knew it was blood even before she rubbed it between her finger and thumb.

"Kathleen?" she half whispered through the small gap. Looking down at the dot again, Sam now saw a second dot a little further along the hallway. And a few yards further another, and another. "Kathleen?" she called a second time, this time a little louder.

When she knocked on the door and it opened slightly more, Sam could see a little way into the apartment beyond. Not surprised, she saw that it looked like a mirror of her own room.

"Kathleen? It's Sam from next-door." The silence beckoned to her, almost leading her inside. Sam looked up and down the hall a final time, then entered.

The apartment sat quietly before her as she stepped through the doorway. It looked spotless from where she stood, tidiness clearly at the forefront of the tenant's mind. There was a very fast ticking coming from somewhere beside Sam and she saw a wall clock hanging nearby, its hands reading 6:10pm. But there was one unmistakable detail that brought Sam's senses to instant attention, something she felt completely powerless against.

The sweet scent of blood smelt to Sam, like a rib eye being grilled did to meat eaters. It was almost hypnotic, calling to her with imaginary fingers that danced beneath her nostrils. The metallic smell drew her towards the middle of the room, silently awakening the hunger that lived inside her. It was a hunger she had felt repeatedly throughout her life, like an ancient yearning, but had never satisfied. Her stomach growled loudly as she stood, listening for signs of life.

"Kathleen?" Sam called once more, continuing to carefully tread around the dining table, towards the doorway leading from the room. She knew that beyond that door was the bedroom, the other door being the bathroom. Whilst the apartments on this side of the building were comfortable, they could also be described as "limited in size".

The door leading to the bedroom was closed and as Sam neared it, saw another faint red dot on the floor. The red hue on the near-white carpet looked like an ink stain, but Sam knew that the color didn't come from any writing implement. Her stomach gave another growl as the smell thickened.

She felt her heart quicken more as her fingers grabbed hold of the door handle. Sam closed her eyes briefly, taking a deep breath as the cold metal felt almost apprehensive to her touch. With a final push of will, she slowly began to pull down, readying herself for whatever lay beyond.

The door creaked loudly as Sam finally opened it. Of course, it did. Something inside screamed for her to just turn and run out. Call the police from the safety of her own apartment and wait for them to arrive. But she knew that time had long passed her by. It was the smell more than anything that kept pulling her along, like a fishing line slowly reeling her in. The hook was firmly attached to her nostrils, impossible to remove.

There was a double bed dominating the room beyond, but that wasn't what drew Sam's eyes. Instead, she fixed on whatever was hidden beneath the blanket that had been carelessly thrown over the bed. It didn't take a university degree to identify the shape of the body lying under the cover and Sam swallowed hard as she stepped towards the horror, the scent almost driving her mad.

"Kath?" she whispered, but there was no movement. The silence was gripping her so tight, that Sam felt like screaming herself, if only to have a sound fill the world again. But just as she neared the bed, the clock radio sitting beside the bed suddenly roared to life, ACDC booming out the chorus to "Highway to Hell". Sam jumped, her heart galloping in her chest.

"Fuck," she snarled to herself. The cramping in her stomach relaxed a little as she snapped the alarm's radio off. Kathleen worked nights; she had mentioned it during their first brief conversation and so the alarm made sense.

With trembling fingers, Sam swallowed hard and reached forward, gripping the corner of the blanket. As her hand touched it, her nerves intensified some, as if warning her of what was to follow. But when she finally pulled the covering back, the body beneath it didn't surprise her.

The young blonde girl, that had looked so excited to be living in her first proper apartment since leaving home the previous month, lay dead, staring back at Sam with glazed eyes.

There wasn't as much blood as she expected, despite the stab wound she could see in the girl's chest, her yellow blouse flowering with the red invasion. But there *had* been blood, and lots of it, the strong scent proof of it. Kathleen Wilson had been stabbed repeatedly in the back, bleeding out through the bottom of the bed she now laid on.

Sam closed her eyes and tried her hardest to ignore the cravings screaming at her. There it was, fresh blood lying before her. All she had to do was lean down and it would be hers. She remembered a movie she once saw, about a vampire that saw blood and struggled to contain himself from attacking the man who was bleeding. That same sense of conflict now fought inside her as she stood over the body, staring at the lifeless corpse.

Sam would later tell the police that she failed to notice the smell when she first entered the room, not mentioning that she'd been trained to recognize it. Fearing her neighbor dead had distracted her. It was a lie she thought she needed to tell, maybe more guilt-driven than anything else. As she stood in the apartment, telling her brief version of events, the young cop took notes, writing each word she spoke carefully into his notebook. The smell of blood still lingered and made the process more difficult for her.

It was during that initial interview that Sam noticed the photos hanging on the wall above the television. Her neighbor's smiling face stared back at her from a time much happier than now. And as Sam's eyes worked their way from one photograph to the next, it was the final one that held her attention, the image gripping her like giant fingers grasping her face.

It was a photo of Kathleen sitting on a towel, the beach stretching out behind her. She was wearing yellow bikinis, a small tattoo on her right breast, a single word Sam couldn't make out. Lying beside her, with its long tongue hanging out, was a Bull Terrier.

"She had a dog?" Sam whispered and the cop paused.

"What's that?" But she kept staring, the beach scene replaced by another in her mind. Sam thought back to the blood droplets by the front door, the trail leading back down the hallway. She recalled the elevator doors opening and the man standing there, a bag in his hands. He'd faced away from her, not turning to see who'd arrived when the elevator doors opened the way most people would. Even when he entered his own, he'd remained turned away, *feeling* for the buttons, rather than look at them.

But when the policeman asked her to repeat what she'd said, Sam instead withheld the information. She knew that if she mentioned seeing the man near the elevators, the police questioning would continue considerably longer. And at that moment, there was only one person she wanted to talk to; *had* to talk to. Tim.

After taking their questioning back into Sam's apartment, the cop continued his interview for almost an hour, constantly going back over the same information. But Sam continued to answer him, offering him everything that she recalled happening, bar the man near the elevator. She tried to remember whether there were security cameras on this floor, but couldn't recall. Even if there were one or two, she could play dumb and simply say she didn't think anything of it regarding the stranger with the bag. Why would she? She was the new person in the building. He could have simply been just another tenant.

After finally asking his last question, the young officer thanked Sam and left. She saw him out, gave him a final wave and closed the door. She'd planned to dress quickly and head down to the MW building. Although it was late, someone surely would know Tim's number down there.

As she entered her bedroom with thoughts of how she could contact him, Sam screamed, the man sitting on her bed as surprised of her as she was of him.

"Shhhhhh, geez lady. It's me," Tim hissed. Sam had to take a second look to make sure the face matched the voice she heard. But just as she was about to reply, there was a loud knock on her front door.

"Ma'am? Are you OK?" the young cop called to her.

"Tim? What, how did..." She held a finger up and left the room. Tim listened as she opened the door to assure the policeman that she was fine. "Sorry, yes, I'm fine. My cat just scared me, that's all."

"You don't have a cat," Tim pointed out once she returned.

"And I don't have a roommate, yet here you are." She paused, then tilted her head a little. "How *did* you get in here, anyway?"

"You left the door open. momma picked up the radio chatter and called me. Said it sounded like you might need some help." Sam let it go.

"Tim, she had a dog. I saw a man carrying a large bag when I got back here and I think it had the dog inside it. I think I saw him." She whispered the last part for fear of someone else hearing her.

His cell buzzed briefly and when Tim looked at the message, read it out aloud.

"It's from momma. She says 'I have the footage, but no clear face. No help here. Trying to track him.' Maybe we should head back to the farm and see what help she needs." Sam nodded and went to her wardrobe.

"Give me five?" she asked, turning back to him. Tim nodded, shutting the door behind him as he left the room.

It wasn't long before Sam found herself again in the passenger seat of Tim's truck. But this time she knew exactly where they were headed and felt a sense of determination build inside her. It was the first time Sam felt like she belonged somewhere, a sense of being a part of something that needed her as much as she needed it. It was just as Tim had initially said. This was where she belonged.

5

"This dude is clever," momma said as soon as Sam and Tim stepped from the elevator. "He jumped into this Chrysler, drove to this here nearby parking garage and never came out." She was pointing at a different screen with each statement, leading her audience across the monitors.

"No cameras inside?" Tim asked.

"Not that I can find. I've tried fanning out to nearby buildings, but so far no luck." Sam watched over momma's shoulder as her fingers danced across 2 separate keyboards, almost at the same time. A fourth monitor was flicking through images, momma staring briefly at each, before scrolling through to the next.

Tim sat down beside momma and grabbed one of the keyboards, now typing his own commands to one of the monitors on the wall. Sam watched with intrigue as the pair seemed to work in perfect synchronization, reminding her of telepathically-linked twins.

"Here," Tim said a few moments later. He pointed at the monitor. "Here's a zoomed-in image from the top of the postal building." The two women watched as he first paused the image, then started to rewind the footage.

There was a 'small roller door at the back of the parking garage. It looked like it may have been used as a private access. Almost 2 minutes passed as Tim continued to work the footage. That was when it happened.

"Stop, stop," Sam called, seeing a very brief blip of something. The rewinding had been going at a significant speed and it only took a split second to miss what they were looking for. Tim paused the footage, then played it normal speed. They all watched with abated breath for what happened next.

The roller door slowly wound up, stood open for a few seconds and then an old silver Chevy pickup truck rolled out from the darkness. It had a distinctive roof-mounted aerial which caught on the roller door, sending it bouncing back and forth as the pickup drove out of frame.

"Can you zoom in any more? Close enough to see the driver, or just get a license plate?" Tim nodded, trying to do as momma asked. But the image looked like the camera had been born some time during the 80's, the pixelation worse than an old video game. The windshield was impossible to see through.

"Here, let me try," she said. A moment later, the image was on the monitor in front of her and after a few seconds of tweaking, the license plate stared back at them; a personalized one with a single word on it: BEATER. Tim punched the plate into his terminal and it didn't take long for a name and address to pop up.

"Colin Turner. 124 Mango Drive, Oakville, St Louis. He's a long way from home. Think we need to pay him a visit?" Tim said, turning to look at Sam. But she was staring at one of the monitors on the wall. It had a map of the previous dog victims displayed and Sam seemed lost in it. "Sam?" Tim whispered. momma turned to look. "Sam?"

Samantha stepped forward and walked a little closer to the

monitor. Something had drawn her in, the other two watching her curiously.

"Can you print this out for me?" she finally said, turning back to momma.

"Sure, give me a sec." After pressing a few buttons, the printer whirred to life. momma waited, then grabbed the sheet of paper as it slid out. "Here ya go." Sam grabbed the sheet, thanked momma and peered at it.

"Everything OK?" Tim asked, unsure of what she'd found.

Sam didn't answer, simply reaching past him and picking up a pen. She put the sheet of paper down on the desk, peered at it one more time, then slowly began to draw a line, starting with the location of one of the murdered dogs, then continuing on to the next and the next and the next. When she had finished, Sam dropped the pen back on the desk and leaned back to look as the other two staring at the sheet.

"What the fuck..."Tim whispered.

"Why have we never seen this before?" momma asked, almost speaking as quietly as Tim.

A pentagram stared back at them, reaching across the 4 states near Kansas City. At each corner of the shape was a spot marked with a victim's number. 3 of the pentagram's 5 outer points touched a location where a dog had been found dead, reaching halfway to Pittsburgh in the south, while the Northern point reached just over the Iowa state line near Mt Ayr. All of the 5 inner corners also had numbers, each situated in a different county across the centre area.

"I think there's a very good possibility that Colin Turner will string the latest dog up either here or here," Sam said, pointing to where the two bare points sat. momma sat down and tapped on her keyboard. Two monitors brought up maps, each fixed at one of the two possibilities, the maps switching to a satellite image to make the landscape easier to identify. Both appeared to be spots located away from urban centers, which made the likelihood of the latest animal being dumped there so much more likely. One point was situated in an abandoned golf course near Mount Ayr, while the other sat in the middle of a field a few miles from the town of Pleasanton.

The two points sat almost 200 miles apart in opposite directions and reaching both was now a high priority. Tim looked at the locations, then back at momma.

"Could we borrow your car?" momma stared at him with a look that would normally freeze water. "I promise we'll look after it." After a brief interlude, momma finally gave Sam the keys to her vehicle.

"Seriously, if you bend my girl," she said with a slight grin that looked anything but happy.

"I promise," Sam said to reassure her.

"Oh, and in case you thought that man would drive his own car to a crime scene, that truck was reported stolen 2 days ago. Colin Turner isn't our man."

───────────

As the pair left the building, Tim stopped the elevator at one of the rooms Sam hadn't yet visited and asked her to wait. He ran towards a desk in the corner of the room and grabbed a couple of things. Once back, he handed Sam a small device. It looked like an earpiece with a small wire hanging from it.

"Here," he said, fixing one to his own ear. "These work like your cell phone. No need to pair it with anything. momma already connected it for you. Just remember that it's voice activated, so don't say anything you don't want anyone else to hear."

"Who else can hear the signal?" she asked as she slipped the speaker into her ear and curled the wire around the outside.

"Just those momma links in. For this trip, it'll only be the three of us." While Tim headed to the vacant field near Pleasanton, Sam took momma's Mustang and headed towards Mount Ayr. The car was an absolute dream to drive and Sam tried her best to ignore the sound of the thundering engine now under her complete control. She'd never driven a V8 before, but had heard just how powerful the attraction to the engines were on those who owned them. Each time she had to power down and work her way through the gears, the purring powertrain seemed to beckon to her, willing the girl to open the throttle again once another open road lay ahead of them.

The drive out to Mount Ayr took almost an hour and a half and given the time of night she was driving at, traffic was almost non-existent for the most part. Tim was still a few miles from his own destination as Sam reached the junction leading up to the abandoned golf course, having to negotiate his way back through Kansas City. As she turned into the drive, her pulse quickened when the headlights illuminated one of the gates standing wide open.

After considering her options, Sam knew the smart thing would be to park the car and walk the rest of the way. Her headlights alone would give her presence away, and if a person missed those, it was almost a given that they would hear the rumbling engine. The sound would travel for miles through the darkness and if the killer was somewhere ahead, she needed stealth more than anything else.

There was a small shed that looked like a telephone exchange building and Sam parked the Mustang beside it, killing the engine and flicking the lights off. As she climbed out of the car, she stood for a brief second, feeling the chill in the air as night consumed her. There was no moon in the sky above and the stars provided very little light. It took a minute or two for her eyes to adjust to the darkness, but when they finally did, Sam entered the grounds.

The small driveway led up to a line of trees that joined the road, then skirted it up towards the old clubhouse. Sam could see the faint shadows of the abandoned building in the distance, but wondered whether that would be the spot. Something told her that if the killer was here, the clubhouse would not be where he'd take the dog.

An owl suddenly took flight from one of the trees above her and Sam froze, momentarily startled. As she stood listening for any identifying sounds, she thought back to her father's training, his words ringing loud in her ear.

"You are the hunter, not the hunted." And he was right. The words immediately filled her with confidence as she remembered who she was and, more importantly, *what* she was. Her mother's suicide note had confirmed what her father had only ever hinted at. *She* was the killer. And whoever was out here hurting animals and killing defenseless women, was a piece-of-shit coward that needed ending. If anyone could finish them, it was her.

With a refreshed sense of confidence, Sam carefully crept further along the small road, then skewered off slightly, heading towards the tree-line. Something small suddenly took off directly ahead of her; a small rabbit or maybe a stray cat. Her pulse felt like the rhythmic drum on an old Viking war boat. She'd only seen a movie about such a thing a few nights prior, the analogy bringing a small smile to her face.

She slowed again once she neared another tree, crept up behind it and hung on to one of the low-lying branches. To increase her sense of hearing, Sam closed her eyes. But the night held on tightly to whatever was hidden in its shadows, not even a cricket out of place. After taking a couple of deep breaths to calm herself, she continued on.

"Sam?" Tim suddenly whispered in her ear, Sam freezing in

shock. It didn't help with her nerves, but she remained quiet enough not to give away her position.

"Yah?" she replied.

"Anything? This place looks completely deserted."

"Nothing yet. But there's a few more places I need to check out."

"OK, but be careful. He could still be there."

"I will," Sam answered and suddenly saw something in the distance. It was a very faint light, the barest of a lick and due to its small size, made estimating its distance difficult. She moved slightly to one side, trying to change her angle a little to try and give some more depth to just how far away it lay.

"I'm going to start heading to you," Tim suddenly said.

"OK," Sam whispered back, her eyes focused on the light source. It looked to be about 70 to 80 yards ahead, sitting amongst a clump of trees. The clubhouse sat at least a hundred yards from it to Sam's left and as she crept ever closer, began to see what she was approaching.

It was the silver pickup she had seen coming out through the roller door of the parking garage. The faint lick of light looked to be coming from the interior, maybe the cabin light left on. Sam crept as stealthily as she could when suddenly, a new voice crackled in her ear.

"Agent Rader," the new voice said. Sam halted, two separate emotions instantly taking hold of her. The first was confusion as the voice caught her off guard and completely by surprise. But the second emotion was recognition, because it was a voice she almost knew. She couldn't quite place it, but Sam knew that it was one she'd heard before. "Agent Rader, answer please," the voice repeated.

"Who is this?" she whispered back, a name suddenly drifting into her mind a split second before it was spoken.

"It's Xavier Ward, Miss Rader. I need you to listen to me. I just monitored a call to the Mount Ayr Sheriffs Department. It would appear that someone knows you're there."

"What?" was all she had time to ask, when something cracked behind her and she heard a new voice almost immediately behind her.

"Don't move or I'll shoot."

The security guard refused to listen as he stood a few feet away from his seated prisoner, his pistol held out in front of him.

"You have to listen to me," Sam tried again. "There's a killer over there and he may be torturing an animal right now. The man murdered a woman back in Kansas City earlier today." But the officer refused to listen. Sam could feel the speaker in her pocket and wished she'd left it in her ear, but the chances that it would be taken from her if spotted were high.

"We'll just wait for Sheriff Trimble. He's been keen to find out who's been smashing up the clubhouse."

"The clubhouse?" Sam asked in disbelief. "Damn it, we have to check out the pickup over there."

"And as I already said, once the Sheriff gets here."

She knew it was no good to argue. Could she take him out? Sam barely had time to register the thought when she heard an approaching vehicle. Its headlights were off except for the small parking lights, barely bright enough to light the way. Her captor removed a torch from his utility belt, switched it on and began shaking the beam from side to side, continuing to watch her. A few moments later, the Ford Bronco pulled up in front of the two waiting people.

Two men climbed out of the vehicle and walked towards them. One was taller than the other, towering almost 8 inches above the man guarding her. Sam had to crane her neck to see the top of him as he stood above her.

"Here she is, Sheriff," the security guard said proudly.

"Thank you, George. You can go now," the Sheriff said, sounding slightly disappointed. He turned and whispered something to the other officer who immediately returned to the vehicle.

"Ma'am," the Sheriff said, holding a hand out and helping Sam to her feet. "What brings you out this way at such an ungodly hour of the night?"

"Sheriff, there's a pickup over there that I believe is a man I saw kidnap a dog." She thought about telling him about the murder of her next-door neighbor, but figured it would involve her in a far more serious crime.

"A dog?" he asked, looking doubtfully at her.

"Yah," Sam replied. "Please, we have to check."

The Sheriff turned and called something back over his shoulder, then held a hand out for Sam to start walking. She did, her escort walking a step or two behind.

"We've been having problems with kids vandalizing the old building over there. One of the owners is hoping to restore this place in the very near future and the damage isn't helping him. I guess George saw you as one of the vandals."

"Do I strike you as a vandal, Sheriff?"

"No, but your dog story makes no sense either, so I'm still a little baffled."

As they neared the pickup, Sam could already see what she'd suspected all along. There was a dark shadow hanging from a nearby tree, the ominous shape rocking slowly back and forth like a slowed pendulum. The sheriff switched on his flashlight and the beam instantly illuminated the horror.

Dangling from its hind legs was a dog, its black fur matted with blood. The scent filling the air reminded Sam of her neighbor's apartment from just a few hours before and she didn't need to get any closer to see what she could already smell. Her mouth began to water and she could taste the blood filling her nostrils. The effect felt to Sam just as it would to a starving animal.

Whilst the rest of the dog looked to be in relatively normal shape, it was anything but from the shoulders down. What remained of its head could only be described as a smashed-up ooze. Nothing of its head remained, except for a few stringy bits of meat, fur, and bits of bone mixed with brain matter. The pickup's front, which sat about a dozen yards from the swinging corpse, had blood splatters so thick that they looked more like paint bombs.

"What the hell," the sheriff whispered into the chilly night.

His cell suddenly rang, Sam watching as he jumped a little. He pulled it from his belt and answered it, walking a few steps away while she tried to see as much as possible. But without the torch to light the scene, there was very little to see. After a brief exchange, he snapped the cell closed again, shoved it into his pocket and looked at Samantha.

"Looks like you're free to go, Ma'am."

"What?" she asked. The second officer approached them and the sheriff waved at him.

"Pete here will walk you back to your car. I suggest you drive straight home."

Before Sam could answer, the sheriff turned his back on them, while the second officer motioned for her to walk. Feeling very little choice, Sam did as asked.

The moment she was in the car and heading back towards the highway, Sam grabbed the ear piece and jammed it into her ear. The smell of blood was still strong in her nose and the taste filled her mouth.

"Tim?" she called. It didn't take him a second to answer.

"Yah? What happened?"

"Cops arrived. Someone called them. Damn security guard managed to get a sneak up on me."

"Did they find anything?"

"Tim, the dog was there. It was just like the rest, strung up and bludgeoned to pieces." She swallowed hard, desperate to lose the taste.

"Listen. I'm about 20 minutes from there."

"There's a gas station about 5 miles from the golf club. Meet me there?"

"Sure. See you soon."

Sam arrived first at the all-night food joint. Apart from a single pickup truck at one of the pumps and a small hatchback in the parking lot, the place was deserted. After parking the car and taking a couple of deep breaths to try and calm her nerves, Sam headed inside. It was as if the taste in her mouth was overpowering her mind, refusing to relax its hold. She wondered whether this was how Harry Lightman had felt just before he murdered his victims.

There were 2 men standing in front of the counter, while a third was behind it. The female attendant was wearing a jumper with a Casey's logo on it. She looked frightened, the man standing beside her trying to put his arm around her shoulders.

"Come on, sweetheart. My friends and I won't take up much time. Just a quick bit of lovin' each." He tried to lean forward and kiss the woman, but she pulled away. One of the men standing on the other side of the counter tried to persuade her.

"Go on, love. Just a quickie."

The first man grabbed a handful of hair and pulled the woman's face back towards his own. As he forced his lips on the struggling attendant, one of the others saw Sam.

"Hey Rick, check out this little rocket." The others turned and watched as Sam went to the fridge, grabbed a Coke and slowly walked to the counter.

"Hey there, sweetheart. Wanna join a party?"

Sam opened the bottle and considered taking a swallow. The taste filling her mouth stung like a hot curry, almost plugging directly into her brain.

"I don't think so," she whispered, raising the bottle for a swig. But as the tip of it barely touched her lips, one of the men reached out and pulled her arm back down. He had a scar on his left cheek and Sam wondered whether it came from another woman he'd pissed off.

"We got better stuff than this." His breath stank of booze, but it wasn't enough to mask the smell filling her own nostrils.

"Just go. Please."

"Don't be unsociable. Wendy here was just about to take us out back and show us a good time. You could join us." The girl looked fearfully at Sam as the man called Rick tightened his arm around her.

"She doesn't look like she's having a good time." Sam raised the bottle again, desperate to rid herself of the taste.

"Yeah well, she just doesn't know what a good time is yet. Give us a chance and she'll come around. As you will." Scarface reached forward again, grabbing Sam's wrist a little harder. Something in her brain snapped as the overwhelming urge took over.

Sam snapped her wrist to one side, the man too slow in letting go. He lost his balance, falling forward just far enough to expose his face. Sam grabbed the bottle with her other hand, slammed it onto the edge of the counter and in one movement, continued the momentum, slamming the bottle's remnants into the cheek of Scarface. He screamed as he backed away, the wound on his other cheek opened enough to resemble a pair of lips.

"Gonna need stitches," Sam said, giving Scarface a smile. He lunged at her screaming, his shirt covered in warm blood.

Just as he neared her, the much faster girl stepped sideways and swung her other fist in a wide arc, bringing it down on the bridge of Scarface's nose. The crunch of it breaking filled the gas station. Sam swung a boot at his knee and he collapsed by her feet just as Rick pushed Wendy aside and jumped the counter.

The third man finally took a step forward, his eyes still staring at the crumpled mass of his friend. But Sam picked up a can of soup from one of the shelves and threw it, hitting number three in the middle of his forehead. Rick stared in shock as his second friend collapsed on top of his first.

"Bitch!" he screamed, finally landing on this side of the counter. Without hesitating, Sam ran at him, launching herself into the air when just a couple of steps from him. As Rick swung a wild fist at her, she wound her left leg around Rick's neck and dropped her body weight down as her other leg hooked around his head, continuing to swing like a hula-hoop. Despite weighing 120 pounds soaking wet, it was the momentum that gave her strength.

Rick tried to grab at Sam, but the speed with which she attached herself to him, and the momentum of the continuing swing, gave him nothing more than a handful of air. The drunk would-be rapist fell forward as his legs tangled beneath him. Just before he hit the ground, Sam continued to catapult around his neck.As he finally crashed back to earth, she landed on top of his chest, sitting with her knees straddled on either side of his face.

The man looked up at her, completely stunned, a small trickle of blood coming from his mouth. Sam lent down near his face and whispered the worst insult she could think of, her rage teetering on the edge as the overwhelming aroma of fresh blood continued to haunt her. If she lost control now, the man beneath her would surely die, his throat ripped open in seconds. But Sam held the anger deep inside her and quietly spoke a single sentence into his ear.

"Beaten by a girl," she whispered, before sitting upright again.

For a moment Rick just stared at her, the same stunned expression on his face. But the words tore into his manhood like a rusty blade and it didn't take long for the scream to grow deep inside him. As he tried to buck the crazy bitch off his chest, she drew back a fist, smiled coldly at him and pistonned it into his face. For Rick Montagne, the lights went out as he joined his friends.

"Sam?" Tim called as she climbed back up.

"Over here," she called over her shoulder. Sam turned to the girl behind the counter, still visibly shaking. "You OK?" she asked and Wendy nodded.

"Thank you," the girl replied, reaching for the phone. "That's not the first time they been in here."

"Well, hopefully that's the last." Sam walked back to the fridge and grabbed another Coke. The taste was now so bad that she would have torn the leg off a cat if it ran past at that point. Without waiting, she cracked the can and skulled almost half. Tim stood at the counter scratching his head as he looked down at the carnage.

"You did this?" he asked. Sam popped the can on the counter and reached for the change in her pocket.

"Please, on the house," Wendy said and Sam thanked her. As the pair walked back outside, a second pickup pulled up and 2 men climbed out. Wendy met one of them by the door, throwing her arms around him and holding on tight.

Tim followed Sam back to where the cars were parked,

keen to hear of the previous hour's events. She did her best to fill him in, including the part where the guard snuck up on her.

"You got caught by a guard?" Tim mocked a little.

"I wouldn't have been if Xavier didn't distract me."

"Wait," Tim said. "Xavier spoke to you?"

"Yah, right before the guard showed up. Told me that he heard a call go out to the local Sheriff about me being out here. You didn't hear him?"

"No. But I do know that John and Xavier both have ear pieces that are permanently patched in to all the other ones. They can communicate with any and all at random."

There was a sudden commotion back by the station's doors as the two men were dragging the assholes outside. The first was Rick and he was still desperately trying to save his pride, shouting abuse the entire way.

"Man, you really did a number on those guys. Certainly don't play the victim, do you?"

"They were harassing the poor girl inside," Sam said, watching as the other two were frogmarched out.

"That's what I mean. Look at you. Give those blokes a false sense of security and BANG. Take 'em out. Freekin toughest victim I've ever seen." Sam punched Tim in the arm, watching as the three men climbed into their truck and took off. As they passed the other pickup, one of them threw a bottle at it. The rear window cracked as it smashed against it.

"Wait a minute," Tim suddenly said.

"What?" Sam asked, looking at him.

"Just imagine how easy it would be for you to play a victim. You know, like cops will sometimes dress officers up as hookers and have them stand on street corners, to catch the guys red handed. You could do that."

"You think I need to dress like a hooker and stand on a corner?" His cheeks flushed a little.

"No, not that. I mean play a victim. Think about it. We have quite good intel on some of these killers. Where they grab their victims from, what they look like, what they do. We get you suited up as someone that might interest them and parade you around their stomping grounds. Sooner or later, you know, we could strike gold."

"You want me to play a victim?"

"Yah, kind of. Although you could take them out, you know?" He paused, looked up at the night sky as if needing inspiration. "Like a victim killer. You play the victim, but are actually the killer they think *they* are."

"Tim, I don't think-"

"It's perfect. I bet momma would agree. If we could guarantee your safety. Keep you under surveillance and make sure to stay close. We might be able to catch a few." He looked at her hopeful. "We could at least try."

6

The drive back to the compound was a little more difficult. Sam's eyes felt like they had weights attached to them and by the time she pulled up out front of the cottage, prayed for her own bed. Tim pulled up beside her a moment later and climbed out.

"John's waiting for us inside."

He led the way, Sam stifling a yawn as the elevator door opened.

"I know how you feel," Tim said.

"It's been a long day and night," Sam answered, watching as he pressed the button marked "BR". The doors slid shut and a moment later, Sam felt the unusual sensation of first heading down and then right. When the doors opened again, they revealed a lit-up boardroom, complete with a conference table, a "window" that appeared to overlook Kansas City and John Milton himself. The table was a round one, so John didn't really sit at any one end. He rose when he saw the arrivals.

"Guys. Come on in." They did, John shaking hands with each in turn. As he held Sam's hand, he said, "And great job on recognizing where the possible drop points were last night. Really well done."

"Thank you, Sam replied, taking a seat. "It didn't really help us, though."

'No, maybe not for that drop. But now that we know where his next drop will be, we'll be watching. momma is already organizing enough surveillance on that field to keep tabs on the insects frequenting the joint."

As they sat and talked, Sam could finally see the illusion of the window overlooking Kansas City. It was a huge television screen, with a picture of a window and a film clip of the city playing endlessly. John saw her looking and pointed at it.

"I know. A disgusting misuse of funds. But it looks pretty cool, doesn't it?" Sam blushed a little at being caught. A man suddenly entered, carrying a tray. On it were 3 cups and a platter. When he set them down, Sam saw croissants and felt her stomach immediately begin to grumble. "Sounds like someone's hungry," John quipped and Sam's cheeks burnt hotter.

"Haven't eaten for a while," she offered, reaching for one of the cups. The coffee felt good and tasted even better than she hoped.

"So, tell me what happened out there," John said, reaching for his own cup.

Sam did her best to share everything she could about the events from the early morning, right down to the smells, sounds and annoying security guard. Both John and Tim listened intently, occasionally sipping their drinks as they did. When she finished, John stood and went to the television, looking out over the city as if it was real.

"That son of a bitch has been eluding us for a long time. If I had to compare him to others, I'd say he's also been one of the hardest to catch. He just seems to be a step ahead of us at every turn."

"Not next time," Tim offered.

"Maybe so, but if Sam's drawing is correct, then he only needs one more to end his campaign. There's only one spot left, isn't that right?" John looked back at Sam.

"According to that symbol, yes."

"There's nothing else you can remember?"

"I'm sorry, no. I wasn't with the car for very long and that sheriff stood with me the entire time." John nodded, looking almost wounded.

"I just wish we could save the final victim." He walked back to the table and sat down. "Tim, would you mind giving us a moment?" He nodded and stood, disappearing into the elevator a minute later. Once the doors had slid shut, John stood, reached for something in his pocket and pulled it out. He aimed it at the vacant wall behind Sam and as she turned to see what he was doing, the entire wall began to rise.

She stood in surprise as another room was revealed, this one appearing much more relaxed than the one she stood in.

"You can't take money with you when you die, I say," John said and began to walk into the new room. It was much larger than any others she had seen at the compound and although it took her a moment to realize, she was gobsmacked once she made the connection. The room was an exact replica of the one at the MW building, including the view via another huge television screen.

"Is this real?" was all Sam could think of, following John towards the couches. He stopped by a small bar, poured himself a glass of something, then held it out to Sam.

"Brandy?" She shook her head, still stunned by the accuracy of the room. Even the view looked exactly the same, a

SIMON KING

bright sunny day outside, just as it was the previous day when she sat in the real top-floor office.

"This really is incredible,"Sam offered as she sat. John nodded, sitting opposite her.

"Unlike Xavier, I grew up poor, so nice things tend to impress me. It's one of my weaknesses and not something I tend to feel like I need to apologize for. Like I said, you can't take it with you when everything ends. Why not put it to good use and make yourself happy?"

A sudden silence fell over the room as John sipped his drink, regarding Sam. But while he may have been looking at her, she didn't feel uncomfortable. He had a way of relaxing her; making her feel like time was irrelevant. When he finally spoke, it wasn't what she was expecting.

"Do you know why your great grandfather did what he did?" The question caught her completely off guard.

"Harry Lightman?" she asked.

"A prolific killer with one hell of a victim list. Why do you think he did it?" Sam thought about the question, a single face creeping out from the shadows of her mind. She hadn't thought of the world of Harry Lightman in quite some time, maybe even forcing the truth from her mind on purpose.

"I'm not sure. My mother never really went into detail about it. I think she tried her best to outrun her memories."

"I'm sorry about your mom. I guess eventually those memories managed to catch up." He took another sip and paused for a moment before speaking again. "I guess my question is more geared towards *your* feelings. Do *you* think he had a good reason for doing what he did?"

"Harry Lightman sounded like a sick fuck," Sam spat, feeling a surge of guilt. It wasn't a family history she was fond to own.

"That he certainly was. But what if he was created to be the killer by the very people he went after?"

"I don't think there's an excuse worthy enough of what he did."

"No, maybe there's not. But the reason I'm asking is because sometimes, maybe a person doesn't have any other choice. They get served up the life they must lead and have very little power over it. Like Harry."

"Why are you asking me about him? I don't know much, just what everyone else can read in the archives themselves, like the old newspapers, things like that."

"I guess I'm just curious as to what you personally think of a relative that could do what he did. I'm sorry if I seem intrusive. It certainly isn't my intention. I've had a similar conversation with Tim about his own feelings, although he does have a very unique story of his own." He finished his drink and set the empty glass beside him.

"Yes, I know," Sam whispered, recalling how difficult the words were for Tim to say.

"He's shared his story with you?" John asked, sounding surprised. Sam simply nodded. "Wow, he *must* like you."

"It wasn't easy for him."

"No, it never is. Not since Evie, anyway."

"Evie?" John waved it away.

"That's a story for another day. Listen," he began, sitting forward. "There are a ton of things I want to share with you, some of which will downright surprise you. But first..." He stopped, looking at Sam. "First we need to talk business. I know it's never easy, but the quicker we get that side over and done with, the quicker we can get you started for real."

Sam felt her stomach turn a little as the words fell from John's mouth. She was never a good negotiator and still felt a little unsure of whether to follow her heart into this strange new world.

"I can see you hesitating. Pogrom isn't your ordinary everyday business. We don't have the same reach as the FBI.

Hell, as far as the rest of the world is concerned, we don't even exist. But what we do here, Sam. What we do here is far more important than anyone could ever understand."

John sat forward, reached into his breast pocket and brought out an envelope. He placed it on the table between them and with a single fingertip, slid it towards Sam.

"I know people expect me to be a great negotiator, being rich and all. But to be honest..." He held a hand up to the side of his mouth as if to whisper, "I suck at it. It's never been one of my strong points. So to avoid all that back and forth crap, both Xavier and I like to make sure that there is no question as to the commitment we make to our agents."

Her fingers trembled as she carefully picked the envelope up, held it in her hand for a moment and just stared at the man sitting opposite her. When she didn't open it straight away, John gave her some encouragement.

"The offer is exactly the same as everyone else. No one is on a better deal than anyone else. Go ahead, open it."

Sam did, sliding a finger along the lip and peeling it back to reveal two folded sheets of paper and a new license. The first had some printed writing on it, the second something small and rectangular attached to it. It was a Visa card, the name stenciled on it, her own. The license had her name, but a different address, one she didn't recognize. Sam scanned the second page as John began to sum the offer up.

"Let's not beat around the bush, kid. We need you. A hundred grand a year, plus a car lease, renewable every 12 months. The card there is for anything you need whilst working, from accommodation, fuel, food, clothes and all the other things I can't think of right now. Consider it your own personal petty cash draw. We also own a gated community out past Mission Hills. The area is perfect for quiet city living and all of our employees occupy the homes. There's one there for you, if you like." He saw her looking at the license again. "That's an address of one of our storehouses. All of our agents use that address on their identification to protect their identity. If you ever need to show someone ID while out on a job, you show them that."

Sam's mouth hung open as John finished talking, unable to reply as the words rang in her ears. When John saw her stunned expression, he laughed a little.

"I didn't mean to scare you, geez. I can make it 50 grand and no car if you like."

"No, I'm sorry, it's just that..." 'Just what?' She thought to herself. It was an offer too good to refuse and the way she had been welcomed, gave Sam a true sense of inclusion.

"Can I take that as a yes?" He leaned forward and held a hand out to her. This time she didn't hesitate.

"Yes, thank you." The pair shook and when they rose to their feet, John gave Sam a hug.

"Welcome aboard. I really mean that. I'm really excited to have you with us."

"'I'm really excited to be here." John stopped suddenly, lightly slapped his forehead and turned back to her.

"Oh my God, I almost forgot." For a split second, Sam expected him to take back his card, letters and tell her it had all been a mixup. It wasn't her they'd been after at all, but someone else. "There's someone who's excited to welcome you aboard."

John removed the remote he'd used for the wall from his pocket and aimed it at the television still displaying the fake window. For a brief second it did nothing. Then it went completely black as if the power had been cut to it. When the picture reappeared, there was man looking back at her, the smile as warm as if it had been her father himself.

The man staring back at her was old, almost ancient from

the look of the endless wrinkles running across his face like a roadmap. His eyes had sunken into their sockets quite a long way and the wisps of white hair on his head were years away from the thick dark mane he once sported.

"Hello Samantha," Jim Lawson croaked at her, his voice sounding low and labored. "I'm so glad you made it."

Sam stood, staring at the man she'd only briefly met when she was still quite young. The memory of that meeting was caught up in a shadow of time, the distance going back almost a lifetime.

"Mr Lawson?" He smiled when he heard his name.

"I wasn't sure whether you'd remember me. You were just a tiny little girl when I met you that long-ago day." His face turned a little more serious. "I was terribly sorry to hear about your mom. She was an amazing woman."

"Thank you," Sam replied. John stepped forward to dispel Sam's confusion.

"Jim here is one of the finest trackers of serial killers I have ever met. While his legs may not work the way they used to, his mind is still as sharp as a tack. If you have a question about anything, Jim here is your first port of call. He has direct access to your earpiece. All you have to do is call his name and he'll answer." Jim gave a faint snort.

"As fast as I can, anyway. I'm getting a little slow in my old age. But I'll do my best to help."

"Are you still in Australia, Mr Lawson?" Sam asked.

"Please, call me Jim. And yes, I am, although I work the American business day, so you'll find me available the same times as you work. If your days go into night, just let me know and I'll prepare for it."

"Thanks for dropping in, Jim. Always appreciate it," John finished, waved and pressed the remote just as Jim gave a final wave and a smile.

"He is one of the most switched on criminologists I have

ever met. Even at *his* age, nothing seems to be slowing him down."

"Mr Milton?" Sam asked. He looked surprised at her.

"Mr Milton? I thought we got past that."

"Sorry, John? Will we continue to track the killer from last night? I mean, we were so close." His face turned sullen as he sat back down.

"As much as I want to end that man, we know he won't be back for at least six months. During the past 9 murders, he waited an average of 10 months between each, and even the shortest gap was almost 7 months. Unfortunately, there's almost very little to go on. All we have to work with are victim's bodies, the bodies of their dogs, no evidence left at any of the scenes. Whoever is committing these heinous crimes is executing them with extreme precision. They know what they're doing and they also know that we have nothing on them." He sat forward a little. "Not unless you have something new."

She tried to run things back through her mind, but there was nothing jumping out at her. Sam shrugged her shoulders, feeling defeated before she'd even begun.

"I wish there was something."

"I don't expect you to crack your very first case within hours. Anyway, there's never a shortage of perpetrators. But just remember one thing. One 'promise', if you will."

"What's that?" Sam asked.

"We never let them live. Once we find them, we end them, however you see fit. No questions." Sam saw the determination in his eyes and knew that this was the serious side of John Milton. Given his history, this was one side of him no one interfered with. Sam stood again and looked down at him.

"I promise."

It was almost 2 by the time her phone rang, rousing Sam from her sleep. Tim had dropped her back at her apartment and after slowly walking past the taped-off door of her unfortunate neighbor, Sam climbed into bed almost immediately, losing the fight within seconds of her head touching the pillow.

There was no dream to remember when the phone woke her a few hours later, and after listening to Tim telling her of his impending arrival, she climbed out of bed and jumped in the shower.

It was quickly agreed that they would get the easy stuff out of the way first. It turned out that all of the agents not only worked together, but also lived in very close proximity to each other. John had only briefly mentioned that both he and Xavier had purchased an entire housing complex on the outskirts of the city; appearing like any other gated community in America. The houses were all occupied by Pogrom employees, something that Sam initially thought peculiar. But after considering the upside of such a prospect, realized that there were far more pros than cons.

Tim was dropping by to take Sam out car shopping and then a look at her new home. Her Jeep was already on its last legs and the offer of the lease had probably come at almost the right time. It didn't surprise him one tiny bit when she asked him to take her to the local Ford dealer.

"momma's car had a bit of an impact on you?" he asked, swinging his truck into traffic.

"Yeah, I guess so," she answered with a wry smile.

He knew just where to go and before long, the truck pulled up at the dealership. Sam barely had a chance to approach the first row of cars before a well-dressed woman approached her, walking with a distinct spring in her step.

"Welcome to Grady Ford."

In less than an hour, Sam had signed on the dotted line, a brand new Ford Mustang already being prepared. The test drive had taken less than 20 minutes and she'd fallen in love with the very one the moment she took the wheel. It was the darkest of blacks she'd ever seen and when Sam had first laid eyes on it, compared the color to her own hidden terrors, the kind that only surfaced when she felt most threatened.

Tim waited in his truck once the sales lady had taken Sam inside and as she climbed back into the cabin, told her the news.

"We have to get to base. John and Xavier have a job for us."

He pulled the truck back into traffic, Sam feeling truly alive with the way things were going. With the car stuff out of the way, there was just the moving part, which she would need to take care of the following day. Apparently there was a house already earmarked for her, one chosen by John himself. Everything felt so perfect.

As Tim worked his way along the expressway, he was whistling along to the radio, Bon Scott roaring through T.N.T. The music was loud, just the way Sam liked, but for some reason she wasn't feeling it. There was something about the previous evening that refused to leave her. It was seeing the dog swinging from the tree branch, the blood splatters covering the front of the truck.

Tim saw Sam deep in thought and killed the music.

"You OK?" he asked.

"Yah, sure."

"How good is that machine waiting for you back there. Excited?" Although she was, the nerves building inside her continued to distract.

"Just something about last night. I just wish there was something else we could do. He's going to kill another person, Tim. Can't we go back?"

"The chances of us finding anything now would be zero. Cops would have cleaned it up well and truly."

"Just wish we had something to go on."

"Did you know her well? Your neighbor I mean?" he asked, grabbing a cigarette. He chased the tip with a match as he steadied the truck.

"No, just met her the one time. Why her?"

"If we knew that then we'd be able to catch him. Try not to think about it too much." He drew on his cigarette and tried to change the mood. "How about that sweet ride of yours? You know, momma washes hers every Saturday; rain, hail or shine. Calls it her own little tranquilizer. I think it's because of-" But Sam's face suddenly changed enough for him to pause. "Sam, what is it?" She looked curiously past him, almost as if there was something running along beside the truck.

"What did you say?" she finally whispered.

"What? momma washing her car?"

"No, the bit after that." He thought for a moment.

"Calling her ride her own little tranquilizer?"

Sam looked down into her lap, thought for a moment, then closed her eyes. Tim tried to watch her, doing his best to keep the truck in a straight line. He thought she was going to be sick or something and was preparing to swing into the breakdown lane. When Sam finally opened her eyes again, he knew she was OK, her words falling into place immediately.

"I might have a lead from last night."

John and Xavier both sat patiently at the boardroom table as Sam tried her best to share what minor detail she remembered. Tim was sitting next to his new partner, still curious. She thought it better to wait for them all to be present, in case something was missed. With a case so precariously balanced, slowly tipping towards imminent failure, saving a single life was at the forefront of Sam's mind.

"There was something I remembered from last night. It didn't hit me until just now because, to be honest, it slipped my mind almost the moment I saw it."

"What did you see?" Xavier asked patiently.

"There was something lying on the ground beneath the dog. I only saw it for a split second, and in that time, it didn't really strike home. It wasn't until Tim said what he did during the drive here that it came back to me."

"Well, come on. Out with it," John said. "Don't keep us in suspense."

"It was a tranquilizer dart." They all looked at her.

"How can you be sure?" Xavier asked. "You said yourself it was pretty dark. Couldn't it have been something else?" Sam considered his question but shook her head.

"One of my friends from Uni works at a veterinary hospital. They often get called out to help with wild or dangerous animals and I've seen her prepare the tranquilizer darts. This was definitely one."

"OK, so how does that help us?" John asked the room. No one answered, the other two men still looking at Sam.

"There's something else," Sam continued. She felt a little uncomfortable, as if put on the spot. "I don't think it's the people he's going after. I think it's the dogs. I think their owners just get in the way."

The room fell silent as Sam's words took flight. It was a theory she only put together during the final part of the drive to the compound, after hearing Tim's words reawaken her memories from the previous night.

"Why do you say that?" Xavier asked.

"His anger is focused on the animals. Their bodies are arranged in a certain pattern and the owners are simply killed and left by the proverbial roadside. I don't think the dog that I saw being carried out was dead, just merely asleep. And another thing." Sam paused and closed her eyes to revisit the hanging body. "There was too much *fresh* blood on that truck. The spatters *looked* fresh, the blood running down as if warm. Now that I see it, I think I remember a faint mist rising from the blood itself, as if it was still hot."

"You think we have an animal serial killer?" John chimed in. He didn't sound like the enthusiastic person from the previous meeting.

"Maybe," Sam offered shyly.

"It makes sense," Tim offered. "Tell us more about this tranquilizer dart. Are you sure that's what you saw?" Sam nodded without hesitation.

"Of that I'm 100%. I remember the distinctive shape and color. It was a dart, for sure. And if he was carrying preloaded tranquilizer darts to a murder scene, it stands to reason that he was prepared for the animal more than the owner."

"What if he came to kill the owner *knowing* there was an animal? Maybe he's just a little OCD. You know, prepared for every contingency." Xavier sounded open to the possibility, but also offered credible alternatives.

"Even if it was a dart, it doesn't bring us any closer to finding this particular perp." John sounded almost dismissive and Sam was starting to feel like he was fighting her on the matter. Not a lot, but just enough to let his feelings be known. "I think for the time being, we let this one slide. We know we have time before he'll strike again." He removed the remote from his pocket and pointed it at the screen. "There's another one we need to focus on for now. Jim had a break in the Goose Lake murders."

Just as it did earlier that morning, the screen first flicked off, remained dark for a few moments, then flashed back into life. Jim Lawson stared back at the room with the same warm smile he greeted Sam with the previous time they spoke.

"Jim, thanks for joining us," Xavier said.

"Hey. Hopefully it's worth the wait." He spoke with a strong Australian accent which Sam had always adored.

"Can you please tell these guys what you told me before?" John asked and Jim nodded.

"For sure." His eyes shifted to Sam and he waved. "Hi Sam."

"Hey," Sam called back, returning his wave.

"Our perp has now killed 4 people, all in the vicinity of Goose Lake. 4 women, all strangled, all dumped into the water, and none sexually interfered with. So far those have been the only similarities we've found."

He was tapping away on a keyboard and half the screen changed into an aerial map of the lake and surrounding countryside. Sam could see a lot of vegetation around the lake.

"The murders had all occurred during the past 12 months and none seemed to be related. They all worked separate jobs, lived in various parts of the state and according to their families, all were straight-shooting good girls. Two were single, while two had boyfriends. They drove different model cars, attended different schools and basically had 4 individual lives with no commonality with each other."

"Except, you found something, didn't you?" John looked at Tim and waved for him to quieten down.

"Yes. I think I found something. It's a long shot, but as far as I can see, it may just be the only link there is."

Jim tapped something on his keyboard and the map on the screen disappeared. In its place appeared a handwritten receipt, made out to cash and listing a single item. A dress, details unknown.

"Jim?" Xavier asked, unsure of the clue.

"It took some time, but those receipts come from these." He pressed another button and a picture of a small receipt book popped up. "Normally they would be hard to trace, given there's thousands of these sold all over the country. But with the evolution of online accessibility to businesses tools, a lot of stores have turned to electronic bookkeeping. These books are ordered in to this particular county by a single supplier: R and E Thomas. From there, only 6 clients purchase the books and out of those, one store was linked to all four victims. A clothing store in Lakeview, Oregon called..." He paused, rifled through something on his desk and picked up a sheet before continuing. "Here it is, called Treasures and Threads. The proprietor is a woman called Helen Chang. She runs the store with the help of her 26-year old son. As far as I can tell, they are your best bet for answers."

"Great work as always, Jim," John said. He turned to Tim and Sam almost immediately. "Pretty good direction to head in."

After everyone wished Jim well, the screen flicked off and the four of them were alone once more. Sam couldn't help but wonder why John was standoffish. There was something bothering him and Sam wondered whether he might have changed his mind about her. Maybe she really had failed the previous night.

"Alright guys, if you're good to go, then find the person responsible and put an end to this string," Xavier said. Tim practically jumped to his feet, shook hands with the 2 men and headed for the door. Sam followed suit, but as she shook with John, he held her hand for a brief moment, peering into her eyes. "Remember, focus on *this* case and nothing else. Lives matter in these instances."

Sam nodded, staring back at John. He held her gaze for a moment longer as if to drive home his message. Finally he let go and she followed Tim into the waiting elevator. She exhaled loudly once the doors closed.

"What was that about?" she asked.

"He gets like that sometimes. He just hates failing, especially when others could die. Once we find this person, he'll be fine again. To tell you the truth, I get pretty anxious myself. From this point on, anymore deaths fall on *our* shoulders. That's a pretty heavy weight to carry."

"I get it," Sam said as the doors slid open. "Let's find this prick."

7

Sam had never been on a private jet before and wasn't expecting to be on one shortly after the meeting. But nothing really surprised her when a couple of billionaires were now her bosses, one of whom was quite the eccentric. "Can't take it with you," he'd said to her and he wasn't kidding.

The jet had already been waiting for them on the tarmac, Tim driving the truck right up to it. One of the waiting attendants jumped in it as she and Tim climbed out, another helping them aboard. Sam felt a flutter of nerves when the plane first left the ground, but Tim kept her mind off things once they were in the air, pulling a laptop from his bag and flipping it open.

He began to open tabs and files and maps, pointing out all the things they would need to know. Victim's home addresses; victim's dumping locations; crime scene photos; investigating officers. It was amazing the access he had and Sam wondered just how many departments Pogrom had in their pockets. There must have been a lot of people involved with this group; more than she had seen so far.

After an hour into their flight, Sam stood to stretch her legs. After a quick bathroom break, she returned to her seat where a meal was waiting for her. The dish looked divine, as if served in a high-class restaurant. The taste of the fish sent Sam's taste-buds into overdrive and her expression must have been obvious. Tim began to laugh as he watched his new partner devour her dish.

"Pretty good, right?" he asked. Sam nodded as she chewed on a sweet potato fry.

"Amazing," she whispered, not wanting to sound like the food amateur she was. Cooking had never been one of her strong suits, preferring take out to home-cooked meals. If this was how good food could taste, she wondered whether she might be converted.

With the sun already setting far ahead of them, the plane continued towards the now darkening horizon. The flight would take a little over 3 hours, giving the newly teamed pair enough time to study their mission and hopefully learn enough to ensure one serial killer would soon meet their own fate.

There was a car waiting for them where their plane finally stopped. After the usual round of thank you's and goodbyes, Tim and Sam jumped into their complimentary ride and headed to a nearby motel. It was an even hundred miles to Lakeview and the pair decided that setting out early the following morning would be the better option. If they left now, their destination wouldn't be reached until well past midnight.

Tim checked them in while Sam waited with their car. He returned a short while later, holding a key out to her as he reached for his bag.

"You're in 11, I'm in 12. Make it a 6am start?" Sam nodded, grabbed the key then reached for her own bag. After wishing each other a good night, both disappeared into their respective rooms, neither hesitating with sleep. Before time had a chance to creep another half a revolution around the dial, both were fast asleep.

After briefly stopping at a 24-hour gas station near the edge of town for early morning supplies, Sam turned the car back onto the nearly deserted road. The radio was quietly putting out tunes in the background as Tim continued to try and sleep after a shocking night. Sam saw almost immediately how bad he must have slept, offering to drive so he could catch up on a little more.

The 2 hours it took to drive the 100 miles passed with little fanfare, Sam enjoying the incredible views as the countryside passed them by. At one point, Tim's snoring became so loud, even the radio failed to penetrate through it. But rather than digging him in the ribs, Sam snapped the radio off and let him continue. She would need him as refreshed as possible. There was work ahead and they both needed to be 100% in order to keep on top of whatever fate had in store for them.

At the same time that Sam was paying the attendant at the gas station, Leonard Chang, also known as Leo, was turning the key in the backdoor of his mother's store. With the recent downturn in visitor numbers to the area, business was bad and that meant his weekly pay check would be minimal. He hated the store, often begging his mother to sell up and move back to Los Angeles.

But if there was one thing Helen Chang wasn't, it was a quitter. She'd survived two abusive marriages, the latter of which left her with a son to raise. After the second marriage had well and truly dissolved into a bloody mess, she had resolved to move both her and her child to a more peaceful life somewhere away from the bustling city.

Lakeview had only meant to be a brief stopover as she ferried them across the state, the original destination being Idaho City. But after waking to a gorgeous sunrise and a perfect view over the pristine lake, it took a single glance for the single mom to know that she had found her new home.

The divorce had left her with a sizable bank balance, one she had to fight hard for. It was the only good thing to come out of the marriage, aside from her child. Once she'd received the final settlement, with her bags packed and heart in pieces, 33-year old Helen took her infant son cross country, in search of a new place they could call their own.

It was Leo's job to open the store each Wednesday morning in time for the early morning deliveries. There were two, both needing to be checked and signed for upon the goods being handed over. The rest of the stores deliveries were usually left beside the back door if they happened to be dropped out of hours. The rest of the goods would arrive during opening hours, Helen taking care of these personally.

But the Wednesday deliveries would always need to be taken care of personally, because one of these deliveries came with an added extra, something unknown to the store's proprietor. The additions were for himself, goods that funded his own interests. Drugs weren't easy to come by in Lakeview, particularly those more attainable in larger population centers. But he'd found a way to smuggle crystal meth into town, especially once he'd learned of the growing demand amongst the willing townsfolk.

Demand always seemed to increase much more during times of hardship and with the lake dried up, so too had the tourist dollar, felt hardest by those businesses that relied on it the most, including his mother's.

While his mother struggled through the downturn in traffic, Leo's business soared, some months moving as much as a pound. But this kid held off living the lavish lifestyle. He was a planner by heart, much like his mother, and what Leo Chang was planning for, was living the high life once he'd saved enough to fund a suitable lifestyle back in LA.

He figured that another 18 months or so would see his self-managed bank account go from healthy to chunky, rich enough to buy him a more 'legal' revenue maker than the current method he was involved in. He didn't like the illegal side of his business. One of his friends had already been busted and sent down to the county jail. Before Stevie's letters had dried up, they told of a nightmare world inside and it was one Leo would do anything to avoid.

But the temptation of easy money was too great, hence why he would supply his merchandise to the needy folks of Lakeview. And he knew that if it wasn't him supplying the town, someone else would step in and supply them instead. Better he make the money for himself.

There was one other side to Leo that people knew; a side that some found out the hard way. He was fiercely protective of his mother. Something as simple as a badly-spoken word was enough for Leo to launch to her defense, often beating the culprit senseless. It was another side that frightened him, because of his temper's complete unpredictability. And it was that very temper that he knew would one day land him in jail.

As Sam reached the town limits of Lakeview, she spotted a

motel on the side of the road. It was nestled a small distance from the road, shielded by a row of trees that were in full bloom. Mountain View Lodge looked like the perfect place for the pair to set up as their base of operation.

After pulling up on the shoulder a hundred yards past the motel, she shook Tim awake. It took a moment for him to realize where he was, looking around like a wide-eyed beaver.

"We there yet?" he asked, wiping the side of his mouth.

"Almost. This place back here looks perfect to stay at. What do you think?" He turned and looked at where she was pointing, nodding slightly.

"Sure. One place is as good as another, I guess."

"I just want to make sure our story is right. We're boyfriend and girlfriend; been together for a year; just traveling around while on holidays. I'm a freelance writer and you're between jobs right now."

"It all sounds good, but you have to remember that we won't be mingling with too many people here. Jim's given us some pretty solid leads, so unless we really need to, there's only 2 people we're going to be following up; Helen Chang and her son."

"OK. I'm just a bit nervous. Never been on a stakeout before." Sam tried to smile.

"It's not really a stakeout. More like a brief investigation. And no-one expects you to crack the case straight away." He tried to return her smile but wasn't sure it was helping. "No one here is going to care about who we are or what we're doing. As long as we don't ask too may questions. Or the wrong questions, for that matter. Let's just go and check in and get our stuff in the room and go from there."

This time Sam nodded a little more enthusiastically as she swung the car around and drove up towards the main building. There were maybe half a dozen other vehicles in the parking spots and most looked to have been there overnight, the dew still covering their windows.

***

Checking in only took a few minutes and as Tim had predicted, there were very few questions, a disinterested girl behind the desk more absorbed in her cell than the customers. The paperwork was minimal, only requiring a single signature and once the cash was paid, the girl handed over a key.

"Room 110. Top of the stairs and to the right," she said, giving Tim the briefest of smiles. He returned it, then remembered he was in a committed relationship and snapped it off.

"Let's go, dear," he mumbled, pushing his way back outside.

They left the car where it was parked and simply grabbed their bags. It was only a few yards from the staircase and none of the spaces were allocated to any rooms. Once upstairs, their door was the second one along, looking warm and welcoming. There was a window next to it, the drapes drawn open and Sam saw a quaint room with a bed, couch and television. The table had an adorable vase sitting on it, but when she bent to smell the Lillies, was disappointed to find them plastic.

"OK, I'll take the couch," Tim offered, dropping his bag onto the small sofa. Sam looked at him, a little surprised.

"You don't have to, you know. I think we're both mature enough to understand the situation. And it's not like I sleep naked." He blushed a little when he heard the word, instantly picturing the gorgeous girl without clothes. Sam picked up on it and began to giggle, further fanning the flames burning his cheeks.

"Maybe it would be more *comfortable* for us," he said, raising his shoulders to emphasize the point.

"Whatever suits you," Sam said, shrugging her own shoulders and dropping down on the bed. It felt a lot harder than it looked and the disappointment, like the flowers, was instant. "So, what's next?" she asked, sitting up again.

"Probably wait until around 10, then head to the store. Should be open by then. Get a look at our suspects."

"You think it's her son, don't you?" The question surprised him, turning Tim's mood south instantly.

"If there's one thing I've learnt doing this job, it's to never prejudge. Prejudging in our line will get people killed."

"I'm sorry. Of course it does. I was just trying to make conversation." He offered a small smile, feeling a little embarrassed by his quick outburst.

"It's all good. I just don't want to see anyone else hurt by whoever is doing this."

"I get it."

"Can I ask you something?" he said, taking a seat at the foot of the bed. Sam nodded. "What did you feel when you sat on that loser back at the gas station? I..." He paused to find the right words without offending her. "I saw something in your eyes that resembled what *I* feel when in similar situations." Sam thought about the moment, knowing full-well what she felt. But talking openly about the feelings wasn't something she was comfortable with.

"I wanted to bite his throat out. I wanted to taste his blood." Now it was her turn to blush, her cheeks feeling on fire as she heard the words come from her mouth.

"I could see it in your eyes. You have amazing control over your cravings. I've seen agents completely lose it when in similar situations." Sam nodded, then wondered if the moment was right to ask her own question.

"Can I ask you something personal?" He nodded. "Who's Evie." Tim looked surprised at hearing the name, looking away as if hiding his face.

"How do you know about Evie?"

"I heard John mention her. Who is she?"

Tim stood, looked down at Sam and contemplated her question before turning away.

"Maybe another time," he whispered before walking to the bathroom.

The pair waited for the time to pass 10 before returning to their car and making the short drive to the store. There was an abundance of parking along the Main Street of town, but rather than park in front of their destination, Tim parked their vehicle in front of a bakery 4 shops down. The day was already heating up and several tables in front of the cafe next door were filled with morning customers.

"Have a bite to eat once we finish?" Tim said as he closed his door. Sam nodded, smelling the baking bread immediately, the scent one of her favorites.

They headed down to Treasures and Threads and took a moment to view the display window. There were two mannequins flanking the window on either side, both sporting bright and cheery dresses. Between them stood an array of secondhand items, including designer handbags, purses, sunglasses and other accessories.

After a brief moment eyeing the wares off, Tim reached for Sam's hand and the pair went inside. She felt a little nervous as the bell above the door jingled, mostly because of the prospect of seeing a real serial killer, but also because of Tim's hand. It wasn't the first time he'd given her butterflies, now touching his hand making Sam's stomach flutter once more.

"Hi there," a friendly voice called to them. It was a woman and when the couple turned to look, saw Helen Chang hanging some clothing on one of the racks by the counter.

She was a short woman, standing no more than an even 5 feet. Her smile was the kind many people found infectious, including the town sheriff who was standing beside the cash register, half leaning against the counter.

Both Sam and Tim returned the greeting with a wave. Whilst the sheriff eyed them suspiciously, Helen saw nothing more than an opportunity for a sale, hanging the last of her wares before heading towards them.

"Feel free to have a look around. Everything's for sale," she said.

"Thank you," Sam replied, picking a t-shirt off a rack and holding it up in a nearby mirror. She had never been a huge shopper of clothes. Growing up with a father in the mountains, mostly away from people, didn't provide many opportunities for learning the art of shopping.

"Here for the gliding?" The sheriff suddenly asked Tim.

"Excuse me?" Tim asked, caught off guard.

"The hang gliding competition. Lots of folks come to these parts this time of year, especially for the Lakeview hang gliding competition."

"Didn't know it was on, but will certainly check it out. Thank you."

"Virgil here used to love to glide, but since the accident, has been unable to," Helen said, returning to her previous job.

The door jingled behind them and two women entered the store. Helen repeated her greeting to the new arrivals as Tim and Sam continued to browse, but neither returned the greeting.

"Must provide you with a bit more work, having the gliding competition," Tim said, making his way closer to the uniformed man.

"It ain't too bad. Most folks know how to behave themselves. Those who don't quickly learn that we don't stand for crap around here." He picked at his ear lobe as he spoke, following Tim with gazing eyes.

"It's a lovely town," Sam offered from the other side of the store. The newcomers were engrossed in a rack displaying "specials", still ignoring the store owner's attempts to communicate. They began giggling as one picked up one of the items, holding it in front of herself, then leaving it hanging on the edge of a shelf. One of them was wearing a yellow and black top that reminded Sam of a bumblebee. The sheriff seemed not to notice them.

"We like to keep it that way. Seems a bit more difficult keeping the nice visitors here with the unfortunate events of the past year." Helen tried once more to approach the girls, offering them a warm smile. But one of the girls held a hand in front of her mouth, whispered something to her friend, then blushed a little as the second girl burst out laughing. It was enough to bring the sheriff into the moment.

"There's no need to be rude, girls," he said.

"We ain't doin nothin," the whisperer snapped defiantly. She dropped a shirt she'd been looking at onto the floor, waiting for their next move.

"Maybe it's time to go," Helen said, sounding as diplomatic as possible. The first girl repeated the whisper, eyeing the asian woman as she did. Her friend again began to laugh and this time the sheriff kicked things up a gear.

"OK, out, now," he said, taking a step towards them. After snickering again, the newcomers walked out of the shop empty-handed, not bothering to say goodbye. Helen Chang watched them leave, shook her head mildly and returned to the counter.

"Don't speak about those poor girls," she said, returning to their previous conversation, giving Virgil's arm a squeeze as she passed him. Sam looked at the sheriff curiously.

"Unfortunate events?" Sam asked.

"Why, the murders of course."

"Murders?" Tim asked.

"Four women, all found in what remains of the lake. Strangled to death." He didn't seem to notice Helen screw her face up as he spoke, clearly unimpressed with his choice of conversation. "You folks really are out-of-towners, ain't ya?"

"Kansas City," Sam said. The sheriff rolled his eyes a little.

"Murders been going on for a year now. I swear, if I get my hands on the son-of-" The door jingled again and Sam would later tell Tim that she felt the air thicken as the new man walked in. The sheriff stopped talking, his staring eyes looking more like a glare as he eyed the new arrival.

The man descended the stairs with a lollipop stick jutting from his lips, gave Tim and Sam a brief wave as he crossed the shop floor, then silently walked around the side of the counter to where his mother stood. He pulled the sweet from his mouth and kissed her cheek lightly as Helen whispered something none of the others heard. He nodded, then headed through a small doorway that led to the rear of the store.

"My son, Leo," she offered as they stood watching. "He works here from time to time." Virgil instantly changed the subject.

"So, you folks going to support this fine lady's store?" Helen gasped in shock, but failed to hide the smile.

"Virgil, you can't say that." He looked genuinely surprised.

"Huh? Sure I can. Just helping drum up some business for you, my sweets." He actually blushed very faintly as he grinned at her and Sam understood that whatever relationship they had, was still in its infancy.

"Actually," Sam began, walking to one of the shelves by the front door. "I do like the look of these." She held up a pair of Ray ban sunglasses, slipping them on and admiring herself in one of the small mirrors that lined the wall.

"A wise choice," the sheriff offered, giving Helen an exaggerated wink.

Sam handed over her intended purchase, together with two fifties.

"So where are you folks staying?" the sheriff asked as Helen wrote out a receipt.

"Out at Mountain View Lodge," Tim said as Helen bagged Sam's purchase.

"That's a lovely spot. Great view of the Connery's stables. They own one of the more prestigious horse studs in the area."

"Yes, I saw them out back."

"Don't like horses," Helen said. "Beastly animals."

"I love them," Sam said defensively, taking her purchase.

"So do I, my dear, so do I," the sheriff answered, giving Helen another wink.

As they climbed back into their car, Sam slid the sunglasses onto her head and reached into the backseat where her handbag sat. After ruffling through it for a moment, she pulled out what she was looking for. After flipping open her cell and bringing up the photo she hoped would settle something in her mind, she held her newly received receipt side-by-side with the photo.

"Everything matches," she said, comparing the two. "Right down to the weird wiggle at the end of the s's." She held the two out to Tim who took them and compared.

"So at least the receipts match. Now what?" But the grumble of his stomach answered the question for them.

The pair climbed back out and headed into the bakery. The crowd outside had swelled during their time in the store and now only a couple of tables remained. Tim asked Sam for her order, then suggested she grab one of the vacant places. She did, sitting in the gorgeous sunshine as the crowd continued their many conversations around her.

As she sat watching the constant flow of foot traffic pass by, several of the voices behind her cleared enough for her to hear.

"Leo had plenty. I saw it when he gave me mine. Just say you'll pay him next week. Trust me, he'll spot you the candy." When Sam subtly turned, she saw the women who'd come into the store earlier. They were sitting at the table immediately behind her, trying to talk discreetly amongst themselves.

Sam turned back, hoping for more, but a second later both women stood and walked back down the street towards Treasures and Threads. But rather than stop, as Sam suspected, the pair continued walking, eventually disappearing down a side alley.

Tim returned shortly after, carrying two bags and two bottles of Coke. He set their food down, sat down opposite and opened his sandwich.

"Leo is a dealer," Sam whispered, reaching for her own food. He looked at her surprised.

"You got that just by looking at him?" he asked, trying to keep from spitting food out.

"No, silly. Those girls that were in the store before? They were sitting right there when I sat down and I overheard them talking. I don't know what kind, but he's definitely into something." Tim looked at the store thoughtfully.

"Maybe those women owed him; the ones who died," she whispered.

"But Jim already said none of them used."

"Maybe not, but what if they had boyfriends? Or friends that wanted gear?" Sam nodded, taking a bite of her sandwich.

"How are we going to find out?"

"I don't know," he said, taking another bite. "But we need to, and quickly."

Once the pair had finished their early lunch, they headed back to the motel. Tim wanted to speak directly with momma and didn't want to hide his conversation while sitting in the middle of a crowd. Once back in the room, he inserted his ear piece and sat on the couch as he waited for her to respond.

Sam sat near the balcony and watched some horses in a nearby paddock. Whilst the mission at hand was nagging her just as much as it was Tim, there was something else at the forefront of her mind: the K9 killer. Despite John's instructions to let it go, she felt that she was close; maybe closer than anyone of them had ever been.

She had, after all, actually seen the man responsible for the string of murders; had in fact watched him carry the dog out of the building, right past her. And if anything, she was positive the dog was still alive.

But there was more to it than that. Why the dogs? The city was full of dogs, so why would he kill these ones? There was a link that they were missing and Sam knew that she needed to find it.

"Only 2 of the victims had boyfriends who used drugs," Tim suddenly said, walking past her and out onto the balcony. "Both had been charged for possession. But the other 2 are as clean as a whistle; not even so much as a parking ticket."

"Then what?" Sam asked as she walked out into the sunshine.

"I don't know. Maybe I need to hit a certain Leo Chang up for some of his finest." Sam looked at him surprised.

"You want to go and buy drugs?"

"Maybe it's a great way in. You know. To get close to him." Tim popped a smoke in his mouth and lit it with a match. "It may just be the only way to get near enough to him," he said, blowing a bluish haze into the sky.

"Yah, sure. And what if the sheriff catches you?"

"Who, Virgil?" Sam stared at him, her head cocked to one side. "Listen, Sam. I won't get caught. But this twerp may just be on his way to killing again. It's a risk we need to take."

She knew he was right, simply nodding at him before turning her attention back to the horses. 2 were now galloping up a distant hill, kicking light puffs of dust into the air as they went.

"Just be careful," she said, before heading back inside. It was then, she decided, that she would do some of her own digging. Whilst Tim was out meeting with Leo, she would hit her laptop and continue her quest to solving the K9 killer.

Tim figured that the best way to get Leo to sell him some gear was to first find one of Leo's already trusted clients. And what better place is there than the local bars. Regardless of a town's size, there was always somewhere for the locals to unwind and Lakeview was no different, several local establishments proving popular.

He left a little after 7, leaving Sam to continue watching an I Love Lucy marathon. He wasn't much of a fan of old comedy shows the way she was. But Sam seemed to enjoy them, laughing hysterically at some of the antics.

The first bar he visited was almost deserted and it didn't take him long to find that it wasn't the kind of place that would serve the kind of clientele he needed. The second bar, although slightly busier, also proved a bust. The bartender simply stared at him when asked if there was somewhere to buy some decent gear.

But the third bar proved a winner, a place called the "The Drunken Duck", which lived near the outskirts. It turned out that he didn't need to speak to anyone else, because when Tim first entered the joint, Leo Chang was already sitting at the bar, flanked by two women, one of whom was wearing a distinctive yellow and black top.

Despite the smell of stale beer and a smoke cloud hanging

thick above the room, the place was livelier than anywhere he'd seen in the town. There must have been at least 4 dozen people mingling, dancing and generally having a great time. The music was loud, some of the voices louder and everyone looked to be shaking their workday-blues off.

Being a very extroverted kind of guy, it didn't take Tim long to engage a group of revelers and shortly after, found himself face to face with the man of the moment after asking to score a hit for the night.

Leo wasn't one for smalltalk, or long talk for that matter, simply stating his price and handing over a small cellophane bag of powder. When Tim said he was taking it back for his girlfriend, the Al Capone-wannabe simply waved him away, completely disinterested in his story.

The entire sequence was over in less than 10 minutes and when he walked back into his motel room, surprised Sam who was busy typing away on her laptop.

"Did you change your mind?" she asked.

"It's already done," Tim replied, holding up the bag of powder. Sam looked at him, unsure of whether he was pulling her leg. "Seriously. The guy didn't give a rat's ass about who I was. He told me a price, I handed the cash over and he gave me this."

"Did you find out anything at all?"

"There was no chance. Once the deal was done, he swatted me away, like literally."

Without waiting, Sam took the pouch, walked into the bathroom and flushed it away. When she returned, Tim was sitting on the couch, his ear piece in. A second later he was back in conversation with momma, leaving Sam to continue her research.

Once he finished his talk, Sam closed her laptop and packed it away. The room was cold and after snapping the heater on, sat on the edge of the bed.

"Now what?"

"momma said Leo had been arrested by Virgil twice in the past 2 years and each time was let go after a brief stint in the local cells. I think the man is a lot sweeter on Helen than we may have thought."

"Arrested for what?" Sam said, dragging the blanket over her shoulders.

"Once for possession; the other for drunk and disorderly. But get this. Helen Chang was also arrested by our esteemed sheriff. One time."

"Helen Chang?"

"Yup. And get this. The charge was aggravated assault."

"What happened?"

"The report said a woman had returned some clothing to the store and was quite fired up over the product's quality. Some words were thrown back and forth, name calling ensued and eventually the women went toe to toe. It was only after the good sheriff intervened and spoke to the woman that she agreed to drop the charges."

"Sounds like Helen Chang might have some anger issues," Sam said.

"I think I know what we need to do next."

"What's that?" Sam asked.

"Return your glasses."

8

Treasures and Threads wasn't due to open until 9 the following morning, the pair hoping for a much needed sleep in. But the sun streaming in through a crack in the curtains eventually woke Sam a little after 6 and she lay silently in bed, aware that once she was awake, the chances of going back to sleep were virtually zero. Tim was still fast asleep, his soft snores rising and falling with regular clarity. Not one to lay around doing nothing, Sam decided to head out for a morning run before breakfast, as well as to give her partner a few more minutes of restful sleep.

She had read about Lake Abert on the Lakeview official web page, sitting to the north of the town. It was a few miles away and Sam decided that a run along the edge of the lake would be fun in the morning sunshine. After quietly slipping out of the room, she jumped in their rental car and drove the short distance out to the lake.

The parking lot was completely deserted as she parked the car and after doing her usual few minutes of stretching, finally began to slowly jog back towards the small path that followed the lake's edge. The day would be a warm one and she could already feel the heat starting to rise.

As Sam bounded along the path, her mind returned to the research she had done the previous night. There wasn't a lot, as Tim had returned much faster than she had anticipated. But what she had discovered, played on her mind. It was as if she was seeing a small piece of a painting, while most of it remained hidden behind the curtain.

Two of the dogs had been related. It took a bit of lateral thinking to get to the discovery, but Sam knew that the secret to catching this killer remained firmly with the animals, despite what the others were thinking.

Victim 4, a woman named Melinda Delaware, had purchased a puppy from another woman, Patricia Livingston. The latter lady would later become victim 7, her dog found hanging from a tree at a local kindergarten, its head completely pulverized, with brain matter sprayed across a children's mural.

She hadn't enough time to investigate further, but found the connection intriguing. Could others also be related? Something suddenly splashed in the water nearby and Sam looked to see a duck start to take flight, skipping across the water as its wings desperately clawed at the air. The squawking echoed through the trees as it finally gained enough altitude to slow its mad flapping.

Sam continued to bound along, feeling refreshed by the clean smell of the air and the near silence of the-

But the silence was suddenly broken as a police siren slowly began to build somewhere behind her. She slowed a little, hearing the wail build in intensity. A few moments later she was positive that it wasn't just one siren, but possibly two.

Seconds later, three patrol cars went screaming past her, each following the one in front closely. Sam paused and watched as they flew past, positive that Sheriff Virgil was driving the lead car. Her eyes followed them up the road until they vanished around a bend. They reappeared further down, then disappeared a second time.

The sirens faded away with the cars themselves and Sam soon found herself alone once more, the country silence once more surrounding her. She briefly considered turning back, the heat already feeling a little uncomfortable. There was a tree stump a hundred-or-so yards ahead and she decided that the stump seemed like the perfect halfway point, using it as the marker.

If she had turned back when she first thought of it, things may have turned out quite differently. As Sam neared the stump, her eyes wandered back to where the patrol cars had disappeared around the bend and that was when she spotted them for the third time, sitting near the edge of the water, their roof lights still flickering back and forth. Something had certainly happened and it was bad enough for not one, but three patrol units to attend.

Sam decided to continue running towards the sheriff's vehicles, despite them being 2 to 3 miles away. As she rounded another corner and briefly lost track of them again, another vehicle suddenly drove past, this one a lot slower than the police cruisers before. It was Paramedics, although these were in no hurry, their sirens quiet. Not even their lights were active, despite the three units still displaying them at whatever had occurred by the water.

It took Sam another 15 minutes to finally reach the spot where the cruisers had left the road and driven the short distance to the water's edge. The ambulance had also driven down, but had parked a couple of dozen yards back towards the road, its rear door open.

The group of officers were huddled around a spot near the

water, while the paramedics stood nearby with a gurney. Sam walked a little closer to the group and saw that a second gurney had already been placed into the ambulance, a sheet covering a body lying on it.

She turned back to where the officers stood and held her breath as she saw the body lying at their feet. The blond hair was almost as bright as her own, but that wasn't what struck her. What really grabbed her attention was the bright yellow and black top the woman was wearing, reminding her of a bumblebee.

Her heart began to beat faster in her chest as she stood watching the officers inspect the body. It was Sam's anger that was building, seeing the helpless girl lying lifeless at their feet. Someone had ended her life and the life of her friend. Ended it without any care or consideration. They were killed and disposed of like unwanted pieces of garbage.

Sam felt tears sting her eyes as she remained standing there, watching with the beating inside her growing more intense. It was a real conflict as she looked on, understanding what her mom must have felt. There was a new awareness blooming inside her, one she'd often known about, but not something that ever came forward the way it did at that moment. It was as if a new entity was being birthed, one that felt the pain, the anger at seeing the victim lying lifeless in the dirt.

This new awareness was another part of her conscious, one that felt completely different to the monster inside her. It kind of reminded her of an episode of the Simpsons, where bad Homer, appearing as the Devil, sat on one shoulder, while good Homer, appearing like an Angel, sat on the other.

The new feeling she was having felt more like needing to avenge this victim, to make things right for her. Sam wondered whether that was the feeling the other agents had when they finally snuffed out a serial killer, focusing all their rage on the person responsible for the multitude of death and misery they had caused. She was the one that would avenge the girl lying dead on that small outcrop of sand, her and the friend lying dead in the ambulance behind her, plus of course the other victims the same killer had robbed of life.

"Hey, what are you doing?" a voice suddenly called and Sam looked up to see one of the paramedics watching her.

She didn't bother waiting, simply turning and walking back towards the road. Soon she was jogging, slowly making her way along the lake's edge, more tears filling her as she struggled to see. The anger was burning inside her, as thoughts of the girl's final moments played out in Sam's mind.

She continued to run, faster and faster, desperate to exhaust herself and subdue the increasing rage inside her. It felt like searing bolts of heat running through her, her brain sending it out into her body to pump her legs harder and faster, before returning to her mind like mini thunderbolts. It was anger, rage, fury, wrath. Whatever one wanted to call it. But above all, it was a thirst for vengeance, one that could only be satisfied by quenching the thirst of her other side, the darker side that slept deep inside her. That was the side that would awaken when the time was right, her own little devil that sat on her shoulder. Only this one had teeth meant for tearing flesh and making blood flow; feeding a craving that could only be satisfied by tasting the blood of its one and only target.

Sam was almost sprinting now, her breathing hard and fast as it struggled to keep up with her legs. Sweat was pouring down the side of her face, stinging her eyes that were already struggling with the tears.

She finally reached the parking lot and slowed to a walk. A new car was now parked there, a rusted Dodge truck sitting a few yards from her own. Two men were standing near the back of it, one holding a fishing pole, while the other was fumbling for something in the tray.

They looked up as Sam approached, both instantly taken by the lonely girl walking towards them.

"Hey, you lookin for a party, honey?" one called, his buddy standing upright on the back of the truck.

"Damn Hank, you seen what I'm seein?" The second man hopped down, landing almost beside Sam as she hurried towards her car. Her pulse was pounding in her temples, but exhaustion wasn't the reason. She tried her best to ignore the comments, aware that her actions were fueled by the raw emotion of what she had witnessed moments before.

"Nice piece of ass like that. Think she should stay for a bit. Watcha thinkin there, Reg?"

The man called Hank suddenly sidestepped his way next to Sam, reached out and grabbed her wrist. Sam had an instant vision of Leo grabbing it, feeling his hand and not the man now holding it.

"I think we should convince her," Reg said, now coming around the side of the truck. He threw the fishing rod in the back and hurried towards Sam's car, leaning against the driver's door once there. "Don't say much, does she?"

"That's cause she's saving her voice for all the moanin," Hank whispered into her ear. He tightened his grip on her wrist some and that was when he realized the errors of his ways.

Sam twisted her forearm so suddenly that Hank had only a split second warning before she was free, the first indication of something happening when his index finger audibly snapped in two. The look of surprise and pain was only short-lived as Sam followed up with a downward swing of her fist, connecting with the man's testicles. Hank groaned briefly and dropped to his knees.

The sight of seeing his friend getting trampled by a girl was enough to set Reg into gear. But both men were still significantly intoxicated from an all-night bender of booze and dope. Unfortunately, the girl they had chosen to target was in the middle of a struggle of her own, one that could end even more severely for them if the struggle leaned more to one way than the other.

Sam saw red as she pushed off from Hank's shoulders, kicking off and spinning herself up into the air. Her first foot caught Reg in the side of the face, knocking him sideways, while the second passed him by, hooking itself around his neck instead. She continued to follow her momentum, the man crumbling to the ground as the extra weight forced him down.

As the pair of them dropped into the dirt, a high-pitched scream escaped Sam, a guttural sound filled with venom and rage. To the frightened man beneath her, she looked to be snarling like a beast, her teeth bared at him. Sam grabbed a handful of his hair and ripped backwards, exposing his throat. The scream of anger continued as she lunged for the soft flesh, seeing the thick vein in the man's neck furiously pumping.

He began to scream himself, then pissed his pants as he felt her teeth on his skin. He was a second away from death and he knew it, the monster on top of him some sort of devil sent to kill him.

Sam froze as she heard the man begin to cry, her teeth mere millimeters from ending his life. Her own heart was pounding so hard inside her chest that she was afraid of being unable to stop herself. The world was still awash in a haze of red as she lifted her head up, looking down at the weeping man beneath her.

"Please. Please don't hurt me, I'm sorry." He was begging for his life. Sam slowly felt herself return to normal, then slowly stood, feeling ashamed of losing control. She looked down at the man for a moment, listening to his cries.

"I'm sorry," she finally whispered apologetically, her own fears washing over her. Before the man had a chance to say anything else, Sam stepped over him, jumped in her car and drove away. It was an awakening she never spoke about again.

"Those girls from yesterday, you know the ones in the store?" Tim looked at her with eyes that still hadn't fully opened. Sam grabbed his shoulders, shaking him again to help him awaken faster. "Tim, wake up."

"Cool your jets, lady. I'm awake." He sat upright, stretching his arms skyward. "What time is it."

"Time to get to work. Tim, the girls from yesterday."

"The one's you listened in on at the cafe, yeah? What about them?"

"They're dead."

"What?" he asked, now sitting fully up and staring at her wide-eyed. "Where?"

"Lake Abert. I went for a morning run and saw them wheel the bodies into the ambulance."

"Sure it was them?"

"Yah, one of them wore the yellow and black top. No mistaking that one. Tim, it was them."

"Did you see any injuries?"

"One was already covered up and in the ambulance, but the other one I saw plain as day. There was no mistaking the ligature marks around her neck."

"Fuck. Right under our noses," he said, shaking his head as he reached for his cigarettes.

"We weren't to know. Besides, now at least we know there's a connection. They were buying drugs from Leo."

"Yah, and when we were at the store yesterday, I saw him standing outside the window watching as they belittled his mother. And I saw them again with Leo at the bar last night." Sam's eyes widened a little.

"See? He was with them last night."

"But that doesn't mean anything. Not to us. We don't play by the same rules as cops, remember? We have to be a hundred percent sure to take action. Because unlike the cops, our action is final." Sam watched as something clicked briefly in his eyes, then disappeared. She had a feeling she knew what that was, but didn't say anything, because if she was right, she would feel the same thing herself in time to come.

"So what's next then? We follow him around?" But Tim looked at her differently, a wry grin forming on his face. Sam took a step back from him.

"What?" she asked.

"You."

"Huh?"

"You. We send you in. You're going to do what I said back at the gas station that night. You will play the victim. We'll send you back in to the store and return your sunnies. Make a scene, get pissed, do whatever you need to. Just make sure to get their attention."

"Then what?" Sam asked, unsure of the point.

"We wait and see. If nothing happens, *then* we try something else. But I think we won't need to. I think either mommy dearest has a temper and doesn't like people insulting her precious shop, or we have an overprotective son willing to defend his mother's honor. Either way, one should take the bait."

"And by bait you mean me." She spoke the words more matter-of-factly than defiantly. Sam had confidence in her abilities and felt herself more than capable of looking after herself.

"Yes, but only if you're comfortable with it. And I'll be watching the whole time."

Sam thought of the girls lying dead near the waters by the lake, dumped like abandoned tires. She tried to picture the rest of the victims, all murdered for nothing, cut down in their prime. The Memorial Room flashed into her mind, picturing a string of lights with a red skull beneath them, all the souls taken by a monster.

But whatever monster lurked in this town, there was one far greater now, sent to protect them, maybe even two of them. She looked at Tim, nodded and smiled.

"Let's find these fuckers."

Neither wanted to waste time and once they had each showered and made themselves presentable, the duo returned to the line of shops, discussing tactics as Tim drove. The plan was a simple one. Sam would go back to the shop, throw the glasses on the counter and demand a refund for the 'less than perfect item' she had purchased.

Just as Tim parked the car, Sam popped one of the lenses from the sunglasses, then twisted the frame just enough to prevent the lens from being successfully snapped back in. Once she was sure the sunglasses were as good as ruined, she closed her eyes, took a couple of deep breaths and cleared her mind.

"Want me to come?" Tim asked. Sam opened her eyes, smiled and shook her head.

"No. I got this one."

Sam wasn't sure whether it was a good thing or bad thing, but as she heard the familiar bell jingle above the door, she saw the store filled with people as she stepped inside. Helen Chang was busy serving a customer buying an over-sized teddy bear. As if fate, Leo Chang was standing beside his mother, also serving.

There were another 3 people waiting in line before them, each holding the wares they hoped to purchase. Another dozen people were milling around the store, some sorting through clothing racks, while others were busy inspecting shelf after shelf of specialty items.

Sam looked around the room and considered waiting. She wasn't the type to create a scene, especially one where it could cost someone business. But she knew that the stakes were much higher than a few dollars of profit. There were real lives on the table and as she approached the counter, took a final breath as the face of the dead girl from that morning appeared in her mind once more.

"I need to return these," Sam said, stepping towards where Helen Chang was handing change back to her customer. The woman looked at her apologetically.

"One minute please. I'll be with you in a moment." One of the customers standing in line coughed uncomfortably, sensing a shit storm approaching.

"Wait?" Sam cawed. "I paid a hundred bucks for these secondhand sunnies and they lasted all of a day." Her words were loud enough to echo around the store and the rest of the customers immediately turned to witness whatever exchange ensued.

"Ma'am, please," Leo said.

"Don't Ma'am me," Sam said louder. "I want my money back. I should have known better than to buy something as expensive as these from a two-bit store like this." Sam felt guilty as she half-shouted the words, knowing that the chances of others buying something at that moment were quickly diminishing. But it was the bigger picture that drove her now.

"Don't shout," Helen Chang tried to whisper at her, but Sam knew she needed to push back hard.

"What else are you selling that's broken? Cheating people out of their money is a crime, you know?" The woman was blushing fiercely now as several of the customers walked out, the bell jingling for each of them. Leo excused himself from his own customer and headed towards her, his eyes blazing with anger.

"You have to leave," he shouted back.

"Right after you pay me my refund." Sam kept the image of the dead girl in her mind, using it to fan her anger. One of the people before her was more than likely responsible for her death and Sam had no intention of keeping quiet.

"Here," Helen said, holding out two fifty dollar bills. "Take your money and get out." Sam dropped the glasses on the counter, glared at the woman as she snatched the bills up and turned to leave. Just as she did, a hand suddenly grabbed her wrist, the fingers biting into her. She twisted back to see Leo standing behind her, his eyes raging as he stared at her.

"Don't ever come back," he snarled at her. The shop was silent around them, the three remaining customers watching on in shock as the two stared off. Sam didn't need to say anything else. She pulled her wrist from his grip and walked out, confident that she had delivered her intended message. Behind her, Leo continued to stare, his fingers still shaking with rage.

"Well, that was fun," Sam said, slipping into her seat.

"Didn't make any friends?" Tim asked.

"No, definitely not." She rubbed where Leo had grabbed her. "Asshole grabbed me by the wrist. Certainly has the temper for it. Think they'll take the bait?"

"I'm almost sure of it. Here," Tim said, handing her something. Sam saw the two ear pieces in the palm of his hand, but these were different to the one she had worn previously. There was no microphone. "Take yours and wear it from now on. We'll have to stay in radio contact from here on in. Not taking chances with these psychos."

"But where's the-"

"Microphone? These ones don't have them. They work on the signals through your ear canal, or something like that. John handed them to me just as we left. Much more inconspicuous. Oh, and they're waterproof."

Sam nodded in agreement and picked one up, slipping it into her ear. Once done, Tim started the rental and they drove back to the room. There wasn't much else to do but wait for a while and Sam had some more research she wanted to do. Now that she'd uncovered the minor link between two of the past K9 victims, there was a very good chance for more.

While Tim fell asleep sitting out on the balcony, Sam returned to her bed and lost herself in the continuing search for the K9 Killer. Tapping away on the laptop, minutes turned to hours as she visited one site after another, following one lead, hoping for a miracle, before it hit a dead end and then continuing with the next. By 3 o'clock, her back ached, her fingers were sore and her brain needed rest. The entire time turned out to be a complete waste.

Despite finding something she thought would turn into a positive lead, it ended with a stray dog that was dumped at a local shelter. She couldn't help but wonder just why someone would go after dogs the way this killer was. Why? Did he hate them?

She walked out onto the balcony where Tim was sitting topless in one of the reclining chairs. His snores were barely audible as he continued sleeping. She watched him for a moment, feeling something inside her. Was it attraction? The thought barely had time to take flight when she slapped it away. That was one thing she had no intention of following up, especially with someone she was meant to work with. It would create nothing but problems, of that she was sure.

Sam went to the fridge and peered inside. There was nothing but some chilled glasses, a small carton of milk and some ice cubes in the freezer. The cupboards didn't help much either. Her stomach grumbled a little as she looked at Tim. He would need food when he woke up and she wanted food now.

It didn't take much to persuade herself to make a food run. She'd spotted a Subway during their earlier travels and a sub sounded like it would hit the spot perfectly. As she grabbed her purse and keys, it was a pizza one she already knew she would get, almost smelling the salami as she bounded down the stairs.

The Subway was only a few minutes drive away and Sam loved the lack of traffic. Growing up in the country had meant virtually any traffic was considered peak hour and this town reminded her of home. Although the town itself had been a rare sight for her.

Samuel Rader had retired from the Navy upon the death of his wife, instead opting to raise his girl. She needed him more than ever and month-long deployments were not going to help the family. So, after speaking with his CO and pleading his case, it was agreed to let him go. But not entirely. He would still provide support on an "advisory" level, often joining in meetings via conference calls.

While he'd been earning a substantial salary for the previous few years, he still needed some kind of income. They'd been living on the outskirts of Denver by then, a comfortable 4-bedroom home serving them perfectly. It didn't take them long to pay off the mortgage, Samuel not one to hoard bills for ever.

But once Judith died, and then the incident with the whole face biting thing, Samuel knew he needed to make changes. Judith's biggest fear had always been for her child to develop the same horrific tendencies she sometimes struggled to control; the very ones passed down to her directly by her grandfather.

While he knew about the collection of dead animals Sam would sometimes collect, it was the incident with the rabbit that had hit him the hardest, Judith sharing the moment after a particularly bad day. She had cried for hours after that event, positive she had brought another serial killer into the world.

But Samuel reassured her as best he could, convincing her that little Sam Jr would never hurt anybody. She was being raised in a loving home with loving parents that would protect her no matter what. And while it did take an effort to convince his wife, Samuel put Judith's mind at ease.

Things would have continued in much the same direction if it hadn't been for Judith's sudden death. With her mother gone, young Samantha struggled with life, virtually imploding when it came to anything social. Friends became scarce, invitations to birthday parties were non-existent and the little girl was most happy when left to her own devices.

Then the whole thing with the school happened and Samuel knew that things needed to take a drastic turn. Judith's fears became his own as he remembered what Jim Lawson had told him about Harry Lightman's first incident at school, one that almost mirrored Sam's.

He needed to save her, not only from the world, but also from herself. The school incident had hit home on so many levels, particularly with the viciousness of her attack. Sam would need to learn how to control her temper if she ever hoped to live a normal life.

There was nothing left to do but sell the house they had called home and move. But not to just anywhere. Samuel needed to take his daughter away from the world for as long as it would take for her to learn. He needed to teach her control.

It didn't take Samuel long to find the perfect location for what he had in mind. A hundred acres of land out in the

Mosquito Ranges of Colorado. The piece of land was far enough from town to ensure the father and daughter would live undisturbed for as long as they chose. Access to the home was by a single dirt road, almost 4 miles from the nearest sign of civilization. It was perfect.

He didn't waste any time in getting his daughter into a routine she would quickly adopt as a way of life. Every morning began with a 3 mile run, followed by breakfast and two hours of schooling. A break would be taken, followed by lunch and another 2 hours of afternoon classes. After another small break, the physical side of Samantha's upbringing would begin, the training both intense and relentless.

Sam needed to be strong, both mentally and physically. With the monsters living inside her, there would be no half-measures when it came to the training. Samuel was hard, training his little girl in every form of combat he knew. The Seals had trained him to becoming one of the top members of the unit, and now he would use that to help his child.

The greatest reward he had as a father was when he faced his girl in combat. Each day he would end the session with a brief face-off, gauging her improvement over time. As the weeks turned into months, he sometimes found himself needing to fight a little harder to defend himself against her attacks.

By her 15th birthday, Samantha Rader was regularly besting her father with the end-of-the-day face-off. The day she finally managed to subdue him completely was the day Samuel knew he'd succeeded. That was also the day he offered Sam the opportunity to read her mother's suicide note, the one she passed on almost immediately, not wanting to face it. Samuel didn't push the point, simply taking the letter back to where he'd stowed it away, returning it until the day she *would* find the strength to open up old wounds.

Just as Sam ordered her lunch, a voice crackled to life in her ear. For a split second, she'd forgotten about the ear piece entirely, staring at the man standing next to her in line. But once she understood who it was, she smiled to herself.

"And a second pizza footlong, please," she told the woman. "Same as the first."

"No olives," Tim snapped at her.

"Sorry, no olives. Thanks."

As she watched the woman finish the lunches, the door opened behind her and Sam turned to see the sheriff walk in with one of his deputies. He gave her a nod, smiled, then proceeded to order for the pair of them.

Once Sam paid for the food and drinks, she grabbed the bags and headed back out the door. The Chang's store was only a couple of hundred yards away and Sam looked to see whether she could see anything of interest. But the road was mostly deserted, with just a few people strolling along the sidewalks.

As she got back to her car and opened the door, Sam did see something of interest. It was a car, parked on the opposite side of the road. Its window was wound all the way down and sitting in the driver's seat was Leo Chang, watching her intently.

For a moment Sam froze, staring back. Their eyes seemed locked with neither willing to blink. But then, as Sam made out to walk towards him, Leo put his car into gear and drove off, shaking his head as he disappeared from view.

"Creep," she whispered to herself.

"Whatcha call me?" Tim answered back, reminding her she wasn't alone.

"Nothing. Just saw Leo watching me from across the street."

"Is he still there?"

"No, he drove off."

Once back at the room, the duo ate heartily, Sam surprising Tim with her appetite. She easily polished off all 12 inches of the sub, then topped it off with 2 chocolate chip cookies. Tim struggled to finish the sub and passed on the sweet treat entirely. But it was when Sam belched that he laughed and nodded his head at her in admiration. Samantha simply blushed.

"Oh my God, I'm so sorry. That's so disgusting." Tim stifled his laughter enough to bow down a couple of times.

"Damn impressive," he said, but that was when his face went blank so suddenly, that Sam thought she said something wrong.

"What is it?" she asked curiously. He held a finger up to silence her, then touched his ear piece, indicating he was listening.

Whoever was talking to him hadn't included her and so Sam sat and watched as Tim listened to the words. After a minute she cleared the table, threw the scraps into the trash and went to the bathroom. When she returned a few moments later, Tim was beaming.

"That was momma. She's already managed to access the police report on the murders from this morning, as well as the initial data from the coroner. They're all saying it's a match. Whoever killed the first victims also murdered our girls from this morning."

"Still think it's Leo?" Sam asked, sitting back down.

"I'll believe who it is when I see them. Till then, we wait."

9

W ait they did and by eight that night, there was still no indication that anyone would show up. Dinner had been a quick run down to a local diner, each grabbing a burger and fries before returning to the room. No one paid the pair any more attention than usual and Tim started to think that he might need to reverse the hunt a little.

"I'm going to go and see if he's at the bar again."

"And if he is?" Sam asked.

"Then I'll make sure to bring him back here." He reached into his bag and pulled something out. Sam sat up and saw it was a pistol. Tim snapped the mag release button, caught the magazine as it fell out and checked the bullets. Once snapped back into place, he held the pistol out to her. "Keep this handy, just in case."

"What about you?" He reached back into his bag and grabbed a second one, answering her question.

"Just don't leave this room. At least in here you have two entrances to guard and both are right here. If he makes an appearance, you can take him out easily. Out there, he could get a jump on you."

He stood, put on a jacket and zipped it. As he reached for the keys, he paused and looked at Sam again.

"And make sure you keep your earpiece in. Remember, it's an open channel, so just speak normally." She nodded, then watched as he stepped out of the door, quietly closing it behind him. A few seconds later, his voice drifted through into her ear.

"Working clear?" he asked.

"Crystal," Sam responded.

Sam sat on the edge of the bed for almost ten minutes as the television silently played an episode of LA Law. She'd considered turning the volume up at one point, but then decided against it, thinking it may distract her from hearing Tim if he needed her.

Eventually she reached for her laptop, opened it up and resumed her previous research, keen to follow up on previous points she hadn't laid to rest. It took more than a little effort to fight her way through pages and pages of information, but there seemed to be a definite connection between more of the dogs. Through the course of her investigation, Sam found that 3 more dogs were related; 2 were sisters, while a third was the son of one of the aforementioned.

But it was the pentagram itself that was confusing her. Was the killer a devil worshipper? It didn't fit in with the rest of the case. Normally devil worshippers left a hell of a lot more clues than what this one did. They highlighted their craft, almost announcing it with passion, needing for the world to know. But this one did everything on the quiet, none of the murder scenes indicating a man needing attention.

"Sam?" Tim's voice suddenly said. Sam reached up and touched her ear.

"Yah."

"He's here and by the looks of it, in no real shape to be doing anything other than going home and hitting the mattress."

"Huh?" she asked, a little unsure.

"This dude is so drunk, he can barely stand up. He's flanked by a couple of guys that look a little worse for wear as well."

"Think he's just biding his time? You know he may just be waiting for a better opportunity. He did, after all, murder those girls just last night."

"IF he killed them. Remember, we're still not a hundred percent on it being him."

"Yes, of course. IF he did it."

"I'm going to swing past and see if I can lay eyes on our business proprietor friend. Maybe she's also a little tired from the day. I'll let you know when I'm there."

"OK," Sam finished, before returning to the laptop.

Tim checked in again almost 10 minutes later, his voice interrupting Sam as she was scrolling through registration numbers in one of Kansas City's many animal shelters.

"One Helen Chang, present and accounted for, neatly tucked up on her couch with a book, author unknown."

"Well that's a good thing."

"I'm coming back. Maybe try again tomorrow."

"My thoughts exactly. Hey listen. Can you stop by the Snack Shack and grab me a milkshake?"

"A milkshake? Sure. I could go one. What flavor?"

"Chocolate banana." He paused as he tried to compute what she said.

"Wait, you want two?" Tim asked.

"No, dummy. A chocolate and banana milkshake," Sam replied with a little giggle in her voice.

"OK," came the reply, sounding bemused. "Be back in 20."

Sam shut the laptop and decided to take a quick shower before he returned. The room had an amazing shower head and she really wanted to take advantage of it while she could. The water pressure back home was always on the lackluster side of things and thus she always appreciated a decent shower.

After grabbing her change of clothes, she headed for the bathroom and locked the door, setting the pistol down on top of the toilet seat. It was right next to the shower and if anyone forced their way through the sealed door, she would have more than enough time to grab it and fire.

The water felt amazing once she got the temperature right and as the heat began to run through her hair, Sam felt calmness flow over her the way nothing else could. There was something special about the way a shower made her feel; the way the warmth almost enveloped her like a perpetual embrace.

After standing silently under the water jets for a few minutes, letting her mind drift into nothingness, she lathered, rinsed and regretfully shut the water off again. She wanted to be ready for when Tim returned, unsure of what the rest of the night would bring.

"Just pulling in. I'll see you in a few," his voice whispered, Sam listening to the sound of the engine as he rolled into the carpark below. She dried herself quickly, then redressed herself, finally grabbing the pistol and putting it into the pocket of her sweatpants.

Once back in the main room, Sam sat on the bed and waited for Tim, her tastebuds already anticipating the arrival of one of her true weaknesses. Chocolate and banana milkshakes had been her mother's favorite and the taste had been passed down to her, the combination almost addictive to her.

But as she sat and waited, there was no jingling of keys in the door lock, no footsteps as Tim climbed the staircase just outside their room. The silence of the outside night sounded eerily to Sam as she sat patiently waiting. The occasional car drove past along the main road, but they sounded faint, the road almost a hundred yards from the main building.

Unsure why, Sam felt her heart begin to quicken a little as an uneasy feeling started to build in her middle. It felt a little like butterflies, something feeling off.

"Tim?" she whispered, suddenly remembering her earpiece. Silence. "Tim?" Sam repeated a little louder, but there was no reply.

"Everything OK, Sugar?" a new voice suddenly said and Sam took a moment before she recognized momma.

"Tim's not answering. I'm sure he was just outside," Sam whispered. She sat forward, reached for her sneakers and slipped them on. Unsure why, she also grabbed a jacket and put it on before slowly heading for the door. Before opening it, Sam transferred the gun from her pants pocket to her jacket, cradling it between her fingers as her other hand slowly twisted the door handle.

Once she was standing out on the walkway, there was no sign of Tim. The carpark was around the side of the building and she would have to descend a flight of stairs first, but given the situation, Sam instead leaned over the railing to try and see him from where she was.

No matter how far she leaned over, the railing held her back from seeing much further into the darkness. There was a single lamp post around the corner, the dim light barely registering from where she stood.

Gripping the pistol even tighter, Sam slowly made her way to the stairwell and began to descend. The fluorescents did their job well and it wasn't until she reached the bottom that Sam felt the darkness again reach out to her.

"Remember, you are the hunter," her father's voice suddenly spoke inside her mind and she felt a familiar wave of confidence fall over her.

The parking lot had several cars, but only one that interested her. Their rental was parked in the same spot they parked it upon their return earlier in the day. There was a Jeep parked to one side of it and an old Chevrolet on the other.

"Tim?" Sam whispered, more towards her earpiece than out towards the car. The silence consumed her voice instantly. The lamp post, considered sufficient to illuminate the parking lot, was positioned on the opposite side to where Tim had parked and despite attracting an impressive array of insects that were busy dive-bombing the globe, it did nothing to help with lighting up the space.

"Tim?" Sam called a little louder. As she slowly walked towards the car, she veered to one side, wanting to see the driver's side while still far enough away to take evasive action if someone was waiting for her.

The driver's door stood open, something she hadn't expected. And there was something lying on the ground, barely visible beneath the door. Sam slowly removed the pistol and held it against her stomach, still more afraid of frightening anyone who might have walked past at that moment. They had promised themselves to remain low-key and walking around waving a gun wasn't a great way of achieving that.

"Tim?" Sam half-called for the final time, now just a few feet from the hood of the Camry. The insects buzzing around the lamp were loud enough to hear from where she stood, but while her ears were trained for any sort of noise, particularly of someone trying to sneak up behind her, it was the smell that finally confused her enough to freeze. It was a very distinctive smell, one she instantly recognized, yet unable to place. It was the sweet scent of chocolate, with a hint of ripened bananas.

That was when everything happened at once. Sam bent

slightly to see what the object lying beneath the door was. It was much smaller than a body, so she knew instantly that it wasn't him. But as she knelt down close enough to see, she held the firearm slightly out in front, just enough for the trap to work. When the metal bar came crashing down onto her wrist, the gun went flying to the ground as bones shattered from the impact. Sam tried to look up at her attacker, but the bar swung back around, crashing into the side of her face. The ground came up to meet her and as Sam hit the ground, the world disappeared into a void of darkness.

The first sounds Sam heard as she slowly began to regain consciousness was the drone of an engine. Her head pounded in agony and she could sense the stickiness of blood drying on the side of her face. She tried to reach up to touch it, but a bolt of pain exploded up her arm, her arms refusing to move.

She was tied up, lying in the trunk of some car and there was something, or someone, lying behind her, She could feel the familiar touch of a body beneath the jumper they were wearing and she thought she had a fair idea of who that person was.

Unsure of how long she'd been locked in the trunk, Sam suddenly realized that if the killer was taking her and Tim out to the lake, the drive would only be a short one, the distance barely 10 miles. She had to lose her bindings or else they'd be dead for sure.

Despite her wrists being bound behind her, Sam had always been extremely flexible, particularly when it came to handcuffs and things. She had impressed her class mates back at Quantico by manipulating her cuffed wrists from behind her to in front with very little effort. But she had never performed the trick with a shattered wrist before.

Gritting her teeth as best she could, Sam slowly began to work her shoulder to one side, while maneuvering her bound hands up the other. The pain intensified the higher her hands went, but she knew there was very little choice. The bones began to grind together as she lifted her hands towards the other shoulder, the pain biting into her, feeling more like a hacksaw blade.

That was when she felt the car slow and carefully veer to one side. Sam continued gritting her teeth, the sweat beading on her forehead as she worked the shoulder to relax. There was the familiar rumble of tires on dirt now and the car slowed more, as if approaching whatever destination it had targeted.

Sam continued working her arms up, the shoulder relaxing enough to allow it to bend back the other way. She dropped the arms in front of her, grabbed the bindings in her mouth and tried to distinguish what had been used to tie her up.

While one side felt smooth, the underside had a distinctive taste and Sam instantly knew it to be tape. The glue tasted acidic as she slowly grated her teeth against one side, gnashing her canines together and creating a tear.

The car finally stopped as her first tear took hold, the tape separating a little more with gnawing. She heard a groan behind her and felt relief that Tim was still alive, although his own injuries were still a mystery.

There was a shuffling from somewhere in the cabin and the door opened. With a final desperate attempt, Sam grabbed a mouthful of tape with her teeth and pulled as hard as she could, twisting her wrists at the same time. Despite the agonizing pain of grinding bone, it worked, the tape separating and releasing their hold on her.

But while her hands were now free, her ankles were still tightly bound together and she heard footsteps, sounding like boots on gravel.

There was a click as the trunk lid popped open and Sam

had just enough time to grab the tape and hide it in her hands as she pulled them back behind her. The trunk slowly creaked as it was lifted, and Sam could sense a bright light being shone down on her and Tim. There was a faint chuckle as the killer looked down at them, unaware that at least one of his prisoners was awake and ready to spring.

Sam suddenly felt herself pulled by her ankles, the edge of the trunk biting into the backs of her legs. She yelped a little, but kept her hands behind her back. The hands pulling her out were quite strong, reminding her of when he'd grabbed her wrist back at the shop. But rather than hold her on top of the trunk, he continued to pull, Sam's head slamming into the metal lip as she felt herself falling to the ground.

She hit the dirt hard, again trying her best to stifle a cry of pain. Whoever had dragged her out was now standing above her, watching as she lay before him. Pain suddenly exploded in her middle as a boot crashed into her stomach.

"Bitch," someone grumbled somewhere above her as Sam desperately tried to suck in deep breaths. The kick had caught her off guard, winding her in the worst way possible. Despite trying to hide the fact she was awake, her coughing fit came on without warning, leaving her gasping for more air.

"Ugh, wha, hel," were the only sounds she was capable of as another boot smashed into the side of her face. Stars exploded all around her and Sam teetered on the brink of unconsciousness again. As she desperately fought to stay awake, she felt something heavy sit on her chest and a rope start to wind around her neck, a thin cord that tightened with each pass.

She finally opened her eyes in horror, only too aware that she was about to die. Sheriff Virgil stared back at her, his face illuminated by the taillights in a grotesque kind of scowl.

"Teach you to treat a good woman like that," he snarled at her, holding one hand on Sam's face.

"What?" she heard herself say. "What are you-"

"I SAW YOU, CUNT. SCREAMING AT HER LIKE THAT!" The sheriff leaned down as he screamed into Sam's face, his spittle flying in all directions.

"How?" was all she could ask before he continued.

"I ALWAYS WATCH. ALWAYS. THAT'S WHAT A PROTECTOR DOES."

"You killed them all?"

"I HAD TO. THEY BERATED MY HELEN. EMBAR-RASSED THAT POOR WOMAN." He paused briefly with the rope, enough to give him a moment of clarity. "She came to this town after a terrible life, looking for a safe place to call home for her and her boy. She came to see me that first day, asked me whether it was good place to raise a child." He paused, looked down at his hands and sighed. "My Aggie had died the previous year. I couldn't save her from a drunken driver." He grabbed the rope again and tightened it. "BUT I'LL SAVE HELEN FROM YOU!"

Virgil suddenly leaned back and brought a boot up under Sam's chin, pushing it away as he bent further and pulled on the rope. Her air was instantly cut off, the vice-like grip tight-ening more and more as Sam fought for control. But he was too big, too strong and she felt life slipping from her grasp. As the oxygen began to subside, something began to stir inside her, feeling like a small flame in an endless night. Something inside her was awakening.

He paused suddenly and looked out behind Sam, some-thing getting his attention. Sam couldn't turn her face to see, but heard stumbling coming from the car. It was Tim, slowly climbing out of the trunk, his head covered in blood. Virgil's eyes grew wider as he became aware he hadn't finished his first target after all.

Not realizing that his hold on the rope had slackened enough for Sam to regain her breath, she knew it was now or never, the wrath now almost at fever pitch inside her. This piece of shit had murdered them all. With the sheriff still leaning back as he sat on her chest, Sam lifted her legs and brought them over Virgil's face, pushing them down as they slid into the crook of his neck. She screamed with rage more than agony, despite the pain riddling her body. He fell backwards, but the grip on the rope held and Sam felt herself pulled up as gravity pulled him earthbound.

His own legs splayed out as he tried to catch his balance, but his sheer weight worked against him, tumbling back and onto the ground. Sam rolled facedown and twisted her feet so the bindings bit into her captor's neck. She knew it wouldn't hold him for long, but it was all she had for the time being. Virgil's feet kicked out as he desperately tried to regain his balance. Sam slid back, keeping her feet hooked into the sides of his head as her body slid along his.

When she was just at the right point, she punched him straight in the balls, not once but twice in rapid succession. The taut body that was struggling for freedom, instantly froze and went limp as a deep groaning built in his belly. Sam brought her knees up, rolled to one side and began to bite at the tape.

While Virgil was trying to cup whatever remained of his manhood's little mates, Sam unwound the final bits of tape from her ankles and stood. Once back on her feet, with her head throbbing relentlessly and her wrist feeling on fire, she stepped over the man at her feet then dropped to her knees, one on either side of his chest.

"You murdered 6 innocent women, you piece of shit. And now you die." Before Virgil had a chance to answer, Samantha Rader finally released all hold she had ever had over the darkest forces that lived inside her. Harry Lightman's great granddaughter launched herself at the serial killer's throat and closed her eyes, letting the other side of her take over.

Soon there was the familiar warmth, the stickiness, as the blood filled her mouth, washed over her face and filled her world as it turned a crimson red. The screams of the man lying beneath her soon began to fade, just like the struggles he knew were useless. His face initially filled with the terror he knew each of his victims had faced, before slipping away into a vacant stare. And as Sam at last allowed her inner beast to feed, she finally understood her purpose in life.

Once she knew that she was back in control and the deceased corpse of the Lakeview Sheriff was lying motionless beneath her, Sam stood and rushed to where Tim was lying on the ground. He was unconscious, and still bleeding from a deep cut to the back of his head. As she tried to pick up Tim's head and cradle it in her lap, headlights suddenly illuminated the horrific scene.

Sam tried to think of a worthwhile story she could tell whoever was inside the approaching vehicle, but knew that whatever she could come up with, would be a far cry from how things looked.

"Tim?" He didn't answer, his face caked in both dried and fresh blood.

The car pulled up beside Virgil's and Sam heard three car doors open and then close. And then, much to her surprise, another vehicle approached, this one much larger than the first.

"Sam? Tim?" a familiar voice suddenly called and Sam tried to see who it was. John Milton rounded the trunk of the car and dropped down beside her.

"Tim." Sam let go as John waved at someone to come. Two men with a stretcher came and carefully picked Tim up, placed him on the carry device and secured him before taking him to the truck. Sam watched as they went while John went to look at the remains of Pogrom's latest completion.

Sam went and stood beside him, looking down at her handiwork.

"How did you know where to find us?" she asked.

"All of our agents have tracking devices. Your earpiece, the credit card, firearms. They all have trackers. We also send a clean-up crew ahead of time. They normally sit a county or two over and wait for either success, or orders to relocate elsewhere. This crew has been here almost a week."

"What happens to him now?"

"Who, this prick? The crew will take him, along with his vehicle and make him disappear for good. To those who know him, Sheriff Virgil Fletcher will simply be another missing person's case that will never be solved. No one will know of his evil deeds, those he murdered. He'll simply...be gone."

Another two men came and dragged the corpse into a plastic bag, tied it up and walked it into the back of the truck. A few minutes later, the car was driven up some ramps, into the back of the trailer. Within ten minutes, the entire scene was gone, including the blood, all of which had been shoveled up.

"Will Tim be OK?" Sam finally asked, the only question that mattered to her.

"We have amazing doctors." John turned to Sam. "Listen, I want to congratulate you on this. I know how tough the first can be. You did well." He held out a hand and Sam shook with him. "It's great to have you as part of the team. I mean that."

10

Sam accompanied Tim to a private hospital in Portland, before catching a flight back home. John said his prognosis was good and should be able to return to work in a week or two. He chose an alternative flight to Sam, due to an urgent stopover, but promised to catch up with her very soon. During the flight, Sam continued to scan animal records from around the country, keen to lay another case to rest before another victim needed to suffer.

The cabin crew were extremely friendly and made the young woman feel like royalty aboard their aircraft. Though not a very long flight, Sam enjoyed the pampering, lapping it up for the first time in her life.

Once the plane landed back at Kansas City, she was surprised to find a car already waiting for her on the tarmac. It was a limousine and the driver was a huge man named Russell Thomas. He held the door open while Sam slid into the backseat, taking her bag in the process.

But rather than taking her back to her apartment, Russell told Sam that he was under instruction to take her to the compound which wasn't too far from the airport. She felt a little nervous heading to base without her partner and hoped she wouldn't be reassigned.

Whilst Russell drove, Sam watched the countryside pass by, thinking back to the previous week. It was her first case and she wondered just how many people she and Tim had saved by taking out the Lakeview killer once and for all. It wasn't a number that could be told with any real certainty; just a guess at best.

Once back at the compound, Sam thanked Russell for the drive, then proceeded inside, passing Agnes along the way. The old woman waved and smiled as Sam passed by, pointing to something for her to see. Sam looked and saw the chimney on one of the roofs. Thick smoke was billowing from it and when Sam looked back at Agnes confused, the woman shot her a thumbs up. It took Sam a moment, but she soon understood.

Once inside the elevator, it suddenly dawned on her that she didn't have the slightest clue of why she was here. But as she reached for the control panel, one of the buttons flashed on, the doors slid closed and Sam felt herself whisked away once more, down into the mysterious rooms of Pogrom.

The button that switched on by itself was the Memorial Room, and once the elevator slowed and the doors slid open, Sam was startled to see almost a dozen people in the room, all turned to face the elevator as it opened. As she stepped out, they began to applaud; not loudly like a concert, but more sombre-like.

John stood in the middle of the room by the crystal column, Bert and Clare standing on either side of him. The word Justice was illuminated a little brighter than she remembered, and wondered whether her cheeks matched.

"Samantha, welcome back," John said, gesturing for her to

step forward. She did, walking towards him and stopping before him, still unsure of the purpose of the visit. "This is something we always do when one of our agents successfully eliminates an SK." He pointed towards a string of lights that were illuminated, 6 silvery stars bound to a single red skull.

As Sam watched, John held out something to her and when she opened her palm, he dropped a remote control into it, one with a single button. She looked up into his eyes and he nodded.

Holding the remote control tightly in one hand, fearful she might drop it, Sam pressed the single button and waited to see what would happen. The music that had been playing briefly paused, fading out like a distant sun. The rest of the room suddenly darkened as the rest of the strings faded almost entirely, leaving the single string of 7 lights left to burn brightly. As Sam watched, the red skull suddenly faded out and turned into the 2 words she read during her first visit: Be Free.

A few seconds later, the room returned back to normal, with hundreds of illuminated stars and red skulls beneath them. Each agent present stepped forward and shook Sam's hand, thanking her for her service. When they were all done, only she, John and Xavier remained.

She was about to turn and follow the rest of the crew out when John reached out and touched her arm.

"Sam, would you mind joining Xavier and I in the boardroom?"

"Yes, of course," she said, suddenly feeling a little uneasy. His tone took a turn, one she related to how he spoke to her during the meeting with Jim.

They waited for one of the elevators to return and when it did, the three of them stepped inside. Xavier pressed the button and a few moments later, the doors opened into the boardroom.

"I need a drink," John said, reaching into his pocket and

pressing the remote. The wall soon disappeared and he stepped into what Sam thought of as the Replica Room. Xavier followed, accepting the drink John poured for him.

Sam had remained in the boardroom and John gestured for her to join them.

"Please?" he said, waving for her to sit on one of the couches.

———————

Once John handed Sam her drink, he proposed a toast, one appropriate, given the circumstances.

"To Tim. May he have a speedy recovery."

"To Tim," Xavier said, holding his glass up.

"To Tim," Sam repeated. The three drank, Sam resisting the urge to cough as the whisky burnt her throat. She'd never been much of a spirit drinker, preferring a good beer instead.

She watched as the two men savored the golden delight, taking a second swallow almost immediately.

"That's good stuff," Xavier said, finishing his and setting the glass down beside him.

"Only the best, my friend," John said. After finishing his own, John turned to Sam.

"Thank you for joining us for our little ceremony downstairs. I know it's not much, but I've always felt the victims deserved some sort of acknowledgement. I guess that room was the best I could come up with."

"It's perfect and I should be the one to thank you. Nothing like this would ever happen in other departments. Just the fact you acknowledge them at all is reward enough."

"Well said," Xavier offered.

John paused, pursed his lips a little and stared at his hands for a moment. Sam watched, knowing that he was about to say

The Victim Killer

something she wouldn't be happy with. He looked up at her again, smiled briefly, then began to speak.

"Despite your remarkable efforts with catching and eliminating the SK in Lakeview, you've also been ignoring my instructions to let the K9 case go for the time being." Sam felt her cheeks begin to burn, aware that any chance to deny the accusation would be fruitless.

"I only wanted to-"

"I know what you wanted to do. But you disobeyed my explicit instructions. I asked you to let it go." He raised his voice a little, sitting forward as he spoke. He turned to his partner for support.

"Xavier, you agree?"

"Totally, John. Our instructions are there for a reason. Imagine if everyone just did as they pleased. Our very structure would crumble."

"I don't understand. How did you know?"

"You mean how did I know you were still actively hunting him? Your laptop, kiddo. It's access is fed directly via our server. Everything you ever typed is recorded." He stood, grabbed his glass then held out his hand for Xavier's. The older man handed it over, wetting his lips in anticipation of more of the sweet taste.

John poured the drinks in silence, then handed the partly-filled vessel back to his friend. Xavier took it and drank as John stood beside him.

"Fortunately, you succeeded," he said, swallowing the contents of his glass in one gulp.

"I what?" Sam asked, completely surprised.

"She what?" Xavier asked. John looked down at his partner, then put his glass on the table.

"She succeeded, Xavier." And then in a near whisper, "Sleep well, old friend." John lunged at Xavier with the speed of a mountain lion. One minute he was standing beside the couch, the next he had Xavier's head pushed back, exposing the soft flesh of his throat. Sam screamed as the blood began to spurt, the shock and surprise overwhelming her. She stood, completely dumbfounded as the two men wrestled, blood jettisoning across the room.

The gurgling cries began to subside almost as fast as they began and within moments of the ferocious attack beginning, Xavier Ward lay dead on the couch, his throat ripped out like so many before him.

Sam stood frozen to the spot, unable to move. She felt a sense of hunger as the overpowering scent of blood enveloped her, but satisfying her own cravings was the furthest thing from her mind at that moment.

John stood, looked down at his former partner and shook his head. His face was covered in blood, a thick patch running down the side of his chin. As he spoke, his teeth were ghoulishly red, reminding Sam of a bad halloween costume. John walked to one of the tables, opened a drawer and pulled out a small hand towel. As he began to wipe his face, several people came into the room and began to remove Xavier, just as the clean-up crew had cleaned the sheriff's murder scene.

"We all must satisfy our cravings," he said, doing his best to clean himself.

"I don't understand," Sam whispered once the body had disappeared into a body bag.

"What you did, young lady, was nothing short of exemplary." John walked back towards her, his face remarkably cleaner. "It was your work that did it."

"Which bit?"

"All of it. But the real break came when I first saw the pentagram. Know the purpose of that symbol?" Sam shook her head. "It wasn't the symbol itself, but rather where it was located."

He removed the remote control again and pressed a button.

One of the screens switched on and a map appeared. John pressed another button and the pentagram faded into view.

"Right there," he said, pointing at the centre of the ring. "Right there is how I knew."

He pressed another button and the image slowly zoomed in to a spot almost directly in the middle of the symbol. Sam stepped closer in order to read it, but John saved her the effort.

"Right there, near Faucett. Bee Creek Conservation Area. Know the significance of that place?" Again Sam shook her head. "That's where Eric Tully murdered Sue-Ellen Ward, Xavier's daughter. He was a devil worshipper. Used to carve a pentagram into the chests of his victims. Know what he did before he murdered her? Had his dog maul her while that prick masturbated."

"The dog," Sam whispered.

"Yes, the dog. That dog fathered two litters and a couple of the pups also had litters. Xavier set out to murder the dogs that were directly related to the one that mauled his child. He considered their owners as their accomplices, killing them with no remorse. It wasn't until I saw you link two of the dogs together that everything finally fell into place."

"But he was here; right here while you were hunting him."

"Best place for him. He used this place as a cover to hide his own horrifying reality. That's probably why he got away with it for so long. But then you came along."

"Just one more question," Sam said.

"Go."

"Your craving?"

"I was born in May of 64, the same year my father was executed down in Florida."

"Wait," Sam said, instantly aware of the date. "You're Floyd McHenry's son?" John nodded.

"Certainly know your history."

McHenry had been a notorious serial killer back in the late

40s and 50s. The official tally stood at 14 murders, although rumors had the vicious killer linked to more than 70. He was part of a traveling circus that kept him moving around the country. He was employed to take care of the animals and newspapers reported that he used the missing body parts from his victims as food for the wild cats. But speculation quickly laid the foundations for a far darker answer, one that saw the killer use the flesh to satisfy his own cravings.

"I don't know what to say."

"Don't say anything, kid," John said, dropping the towel on the bloodied couch. "Tomorrow will be a new day and the only thing we can be sure of is that the killers will still be out there."

There was a second ceremony in the Memorial Room later that day, while Xavier Ward's body was cremated. His remains were boxed up and transported to sea, where they were dispersed like all the rest of them.

Sam was given the honor again, pressing the button to free the souls, but she declined, handing the honor back to John. Once the brief meeting was over, a few of the other agents surrounded Sam, with questions coming thick and fast, while John returned home.

While Tim continued to recover, Sam began to make the move from her apartment into the home John Milton had selected for her. It came completely furnished and even included a ready-made second bedroom for when Samuel visited.

By the time Tim returned from Portland, Sam was an old arrival at the home complex she now shared with the rest of them. There was the occasional dinner party, despite her untrained cooking skills, but more often than not, the compliments came freely.

But regardless of how happy their little community was, all of them knew that their work would never be complete, the memorial room an endless reminder of the importance of their role. With a new agent in their ranks, and a leader that was relentless in his pursuit of SK's, Pogrom was about to kick things into high gear.

Sam knew that she had found her place in the world and that no matter how much her mother feared bringing her into it, she was about to release her own brand of justice upon it, because killing isn't always a bad thing. Sometimes, it's a necessity.

Thank you so much for reading The Victim Killer. Ready for more? Read the thrilling first chapter of Book 2, Body Switch, right now with a special preview on the next page. With each murder leaving two bodies, will Sam find the killer, or is this one hunting her instead?

PREVIEW BOOK 2

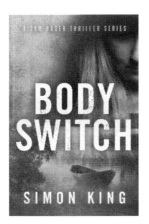

Marlena Perez loved photography. Ever since she was a little girl, the art of capturing frozen moments of time had intrigued her to such an extent, that it became a part of her daily routine. It was her father that had first introduced her to the craft, gifting his child a simple point-and-shoot Canon on her 10th birthday. That had been back in the day when film still ruled and digital was still decades into the future.

Each morning, the mom of 3 teenagers would jump in her car before dawn and drive to a place she'd selected the previous evening. Photographing sunsets had become somewhat of a new fascination after their previous family vacation down in Florida. Walking the gorgeous beaches of Venice, after capturing incredible sunsets, had given her a new sense of direction.

Whilst pristine beaches, like those found in Florida, weren't easy to come by in Ellsworth, Maine, Marlena began to explore the natural beauty she *did* have access to. The hills, forests and lakes were proving to be a true find, one she never considered prior to that Florida trip. Photography had begun to slowly drift from her daily routine before that vacation, but now with a new subject matter to keep her occupied, the ideas flowed thick and fast.

As she pulled into the still-dark carpark, almost an hour before the expected sunrise time, Eagle Lake sat bathed in moonlight behind her. She'd meant to come a little earlier this morning, wanting to catch a few shots of the lake with a full moon above it. The spot she'd chosen sat on the northern edge, a carpark located perfectly within walking distance to the lakeside.

Marlena parked her Honda in the empty carpark, grabbed her jacket and stepped out into the chilly October morning. A slight wind was blowing and as she slipped into her coat, was thankful to have remembered her woolen cap, sliding it onto her head before grabbing her camera bag and tripod.

The beauty of the spot she'd chosen was that it sat at the head of the lake, giving the keen photographer easy access to not one, but three sides of the water. This would prove especially useful when taking photos of the moon, the sunrise, as well as the lake with varying degrees of light.

Once her car was locked, Marlena slung her camera bag over her shoulder, gripped the tripod tight and slowly walked back towards the road. There was no traffic, not even the wildlife making their presence known. Silence hung heavy across the park, with only the stars sparkling in the night sky above.

The track she'd spotted on the map the night before, sat directly ahead and the lonely woman quickly crossed the road. Despite knowing there was no traffic to speak of, the dark still held a certain fear for her and she didn't want to get caught in the middle of the road, should a car suddenly come speeding around the closest bend.

As Marlena reached the other side, the track faded into the darkness beyond. The trees gently swayed above her as the wind slowly rose and fell, like the waves of an incoming tide. Something suddenly fluttered beside her and she froze as the sound crashed through the densely-littered forest floor. A rabbit maybe? Something sounding like a whistling began a few yards above her and Marlena nearly dropped her tripod. Instead, she gripped it tighter, waiting for the footfalls that would no doubt happen next, as someone came rushing towards her.

But no-one came, the wind silently continuing to fan the finer branches above her head. After standing in the near-darkness for a moment longer, convincing herself that she was in fact all alone, Marlena continued on towards the first spot she'd previously selected. It lay at the very head of the lake, giving the amateur photographer a clear shot across the entire length of the water.

The faint waves lapped the edge of the lake as she stopped on the trail and set up her equipment. Having used the camera for several years and knowing the layout like the back of her hand, there was no need for light, Marlena clicking the camera atop her tripod and then selecting the various controls she needed.

It didn't take long for a dozen or so images to get snapped,

SIMON KING

each capturing both the mood and the emotion of the moment perfectly. There was just enough height in the images to allow some of the fading stars into the shot.

Smiling to herself as she previewed each photo, Marlena picked up the tripod with the camera still fixed and began to make her way around to the other side of the water. Moon shots were great, but the sky was beginning to lighten and the sunrise is what she had really come for. It was where her so called "money shot" lay and wasting time on this side of the lake might prove to delay her too long.

Walking briskly with the tripod slung over her shoulder like a soldier on guard duty, Marlena walked back around the head of the lake, following the narrow footpath in the diminishing moonlight.

She suddenly heard footsteps approaching from ahead and looked up to see someone jogging towards her. It was a man, wearing sweatpants and a hooded jumper.

"Mornin," the man said as he passed her, not bothering to slow for her response. Marlena looked over her shoulder to ensure he didn't turn and try and jump her from behind. She knew that the damn rapists loved these types of trails, to grab unsuspecting women who were walking around on their own. She gripped her tripod a little tighter as the man bounded into the shadows, continuing his run along the lake's edge.

Ten minutes later, Marlena paused by a great spot on the western side of the lake. There were two benches just up ahead and she figured it would be a great place to sit and wait for the right moment to send her camera into a torrent of clicks. Sunrise photography took patience and timing. If either one wasn't perfect, the resulting imagery could be completely ruined.

She would later tell the police that it was probably because she had her attention focused more on the lake that she didn't notice the man sitting on the second bench. As she neared the first one, the second was maybe two dozen yards further along, still enveloped in the last remnants of nightfall. The sky was already beginning to lighten and she was now racing time itself to get into position.

Once the camera was finally in place, pointed at the ever-brightening eastern horizon, she returned to the bench and sat for a moment. That was when she spotted the distant figure sitting on the other bench.

The person looked to have something wrapped around themselves, which she didn't find surprising. The mist was still blowing out from her own mouth with each exhale, proof of just how cold the morning really was. As Marlena stood and prepared her camera for the approaching sunrise, she stole another look across at the lonely figure.

She now saw that he, or she, had in fact a dark blanket wrapped around themselves. Nothing looked out of place as such, but that was the first time she sensed that something might be wrong. Despite already being there a good ten minutes, it appeared to her as if the stranger hadn't moved at all. They appeared exactly as when she had first noticed them, sitting back against the bench itself, the blanket bound tightly around themselves.

Marlena looked up at the horizon and saw the sky brighten at a rapid rate, night now completely consumed by the birthing of the new day. She held the cable release in her hand and stole another glance at the stranger, trying to ignore the sense of something wrong.

"They're asleep," she finally whispered to herself. "That's why they haven't moved." It felt like the perfect answer and made the most sense to her. It was a public bench and people often spent nights out by the lake. Maybe the person had a bit too much to drink and decided to sleep it off here rather than risk the drive home.

She looked back towards the horizon and watched as the

inevitable break of sunlight was now just seconds away. Gripping the cable release firmly, Marlena watched and held her breath as the moment approached, second by second, closer and closer. Moments before the golden eruption shot out across the valley, the camera whirred into life, the shutter snapping open and closed in rapid succession as the sun broke across the distant hills, birthing another beautiful fall day into existence.

Marlena smiled as the camera continued to snap image after image, the run of photos no doubt containing the one she would ultimately keep. The sun continued to climb, first just a small sliver appearing over the crest of the hill, then more as it continued to launch itself into the sky. And throughout its ascension, Marlena continued to shoot.

It was only once the camera fell into silence that a thought sprang into her mind, one that instantly chilled her blood.

"What if it is a woman?" She stole another glance at the lonely figure, still wrapped tightly in its covering. *"What if she had been attacked and was now trying to hide from the world? Afraid to move for fear of being discovered."* There was still no hint of movement, a sign that the person may have still been asleep. Marlena turned back to her camera, looked at the sun and saw that it had already cleared the treetops, continuing to rise into the bright blue heavens above. It was now much too high to put to good use in her photography.

She snapped the lever on her tripod and pulled the camera free. As she carefully set it inside her bag, another runner approached from the North, this one dressed similar to the first, with the addition of headphones. He waved as he passed and Marlena returned the gesture, adding her own smile to the exchange.

Once the runner had passed the covered figure, Marlena folded up her tripod and snapped it onto the side of her camera bag. Taking one final look at her silent witness, she turned back towards the carpark.

But after just a couple of steps, she stopped. Another thought struck her, this one another possibility.

"What if that woman had run away from home because of an abusive relationship?" The thought hit much closer to home as she turned and looked back again, her own sister now appearing in her mind. Hope had been married to her husband a little over a year before the abuse started, escalating quickly into an almost daily ritual of verbal attacks and violence.

It took a miracle to save her life, with Hope ending up in the hospital after one particularly bad beating. Harry had been arrested after that assault, leaving Hope broke, pregnant and alone. It took months to set her up somewhere where her husband wouldn't find her and after he overdosed in prison, the job became much easier.

Marlena decided that she needed to make sure the person was OK, especially if it really was a woman. Gripping her bag tight, she turned back and slowly began to walk towards the lonely figure, still sitting motionless on the bench. Marlena looked up and down the path, this time hoping for someone to be passing her part of the world. But the path was empty as far as she could see, both directions sitting silently with a very faint mist suspended in the air above.

Her stomach felt heavier with each step, growing tighter as she neared the person. She slowed a little, hoping to hear a light snoring, or anything to indicate life. It sat completely motionless, the blanket looking old and worn.

The first thing that indicated the sex of the person to Marlena, were the shoes, the shiny black leather looking brand new. They were men's shoes and as she stared at them, felt a slight bit of relief that the person wasn't a woman after all, the whole domestic violence train of thought instantly disappearing from her mind.

What was it then? Some drunk? Someone out to watch the sunrise just as she had, only the wait was too much and the unfortunate person had fallen asleep? Marlena slowly advanced, now just a few feet from the man.

She suddenly decided that approaching from the side, unable to see the person's face, might scare him, a stranger suddenly appearing. She would be better approaching head on, at least from a few yards away, giving the man advance warning in case he woke.

Marlena began to step sideways, starting to circle the man instead, watching for any sign of movement. But there was none, the figure sitting silently beneath their make-shift shelter. As the face slowly emerged from the shadows of the blanket, she could make out his calm stature and kind lines. The sun was behind her and it was her own shadow that kept the man's face mostly hidden in darkness. From where she stood, he did appear asleep, his eyes closed. Or maybe he'd just been shielding them from the harsh morning light. There was something hanging from his mouth, looking like an unlit cigar.

But as Marlena stepped slightly to one side, allowing the sunlight to fully light up the face of her mysterious companion, it was her scream that pierced the morning air, rising like the birds that suddenly took flight around her. Because the face that stared back at her wasn't one that would ever wake again, the instant realization clamping her stomach in horror.

The man was dead, of that she was instantly sure. His eyes were sunken deep into their hollows, his skin blotchy with the telltale blue of death. But it was his eternal smile that would go on to haunt her dreams for a long time to come. A critter had tried to make a meal of the man's lips during the night. The top lip was missing, along with most of the right cheek, the teeth staring back at her in an eternal smile. The bottom lip had been torn and was dangling from a bit of sinew, completing the smile in near entirety. And as her second scream rose above the first, a Spruce took flight into the bright fall sky, wondering what all the fuss was about.

———

The police responded to the call for help from Robert MacKenzie shortly after 6am that morning, two patrol cars attending the scene. Paramedics arrived shortly later and first helped an extremely affected Marlena Perez. She was eventually calmed enough to provide a brief statement, before being transferred to the nearest hospital for observations.

One of the attending officers soon called for a detective to come and see what he first described as a possible prank. The paramedics had confirmed that the male victim appeared to have been deceased for some time. How he happened to be where he was found would prove to be the real mystery.

Detectives John Le Cruz and Dale Watson attended the scene and after conducting an extensive search of the immediate area with the other law enforcement officers, took what little information they were able to gather, back to the station. The body of the mystery man was taken back to the morgue at Bar Harbor, while the officers set about to identify him.

The process wasn't as difficult as first thought, taking a little over an hour after the officers returned to the station. It turned out that the deceased man's fingerprints were in the database. He'd been arrested for two DUI offenses back in the late 80s. The name that popped up was Nathanial Johns, but once Detective Watson entered the name into the system, found himself with more questions than answers.

"He's dead," Dale told his partner as he looked up from his monitor. John stared back at him confused.

"Who, the stiff? Think that has already been established, champ."

"No, I mean he's actually dead. Nathanial Johns, died 2

weeks ago in Danville, Kentucky. His wife..." He paused, checked another screen on his monitor, then continued. "His wife, Doris, buried him last week." The officer looked up from his screen appearing somewhat dumbfounded.

"So what the hell is he doing here?"

After a quick phone call to the morgue where Nathanial Johns was held, a photograph of the deceased man soon dropped into his mailbox and after triple checking photos of him with those of the ones in his file, the two detectives soon realized that the men were one and the same. 74-year old Nathanial Johns, formerly of Danville, Kentucky, who once walked 14 miles through the pouring rain to ensure he didn't miss his 30th wedding anniversary dinner with his wife, had somehow managed to travel almost a thousand miles from his grave.

After confirming the details for a fourth time, the detectives finally made the call to Kentucky. While it wasn't an easy call to make, *taking* the call proved to be much harder. The deputy who answered their call at first believed he was the target of a prank call, initially discounting what the detectives were trying to share with him.

But once he double checked his own records and discovered the truth, his confusion quickly turned to dread as he realized what needed to be done. There was only one thing for it. Someone would need to check the grave.

After hanging up from the detectives with a promise to inform them of his own investigation, Deputy Wayne Dooley went and spoke with his boss, persuading the man with the photo of the deceased man currently lying in a Maine morgue.

A short while later, Dooley hopped in his patrol car and headed out toward Spears Creek Cemetery, situated out on

Route 33. The rain had been falling steadily all morning, but now that he was out in it, it felt to have increased in its ferocity.

The road resembled a waterway more than a hardtop and the young constable carefully navigated his way across the thick sheets of water. Traffic was fairly light for the day and it didn't take him long before reaching the cemetery's outer gate. It was closed, but visitors were able to walk through the narrow turnstile, installed to keep vehicles out.

Looking out through his window, Dooley could see that the rain had no intention of letting up despite his urgent assignment and thus reached for his hat, slipped it on his head and pulled it down a little tighter for extra protection. Rain or no rain, this was one job he needed to do, even if just to satisfy his own curiosity.

As he hopped out of his car, he pulled his collar up a little higher, trying his best to limit the space between his jacket and hat. The wind was strong enough to push the rain sideways and his face was drenched before he'd walked more than a few yards. Once he reached the gate, he dropped his shoulders and gave in, resounding himself to the fact he was going to get wet no matter what.

The wind was sprinting across the cemetery, sending the trees whipping back and forth as Dooley first went to the information map to locate the exact spot of Mr. Johns. With any luck, it would be near the front, limiting the time he needed to confirm that the grave lay undisturbed, no doubt with the finely resting corpse beneath several feet of fine Kentucky dirt.

He ran his finger along the names on the board, silently ticking each off. Finally, the mental list dinged as the name above his finger matched his mental check list.According to the map, Nathanial Johns was resting at home in row L, plot number 42.

Squinting into the rain once more, Dooley began to head towards the path leading up the middle of the grounds, reducing the need for him to walk further than necessary. He looked at some of the tombstones as he passed, silently reading the names in his mind. As he read someone with the first name 'Wayne', he suddenly realized that the names on these markers were of real people, those who had run the course of their lives and ended up here, at Remingtons, until whatever happened in eternity.

A chill suddenly ran down his spine and an uncontrolled shiver shook him lightly as he quickened his step. Remaining in the cemetery any longer than he needed to suddenly wasn't at the top of his list. He peered across the rows again, hoping to find the grave, confirm its undisturbed nature and return to the relative comfort of his patrol car.

The sign signifying row L lay just ahead, two arrows beneath pointing in opposite directions. To his left lay those in plots 1 to 25, to his right, 26 to 50. Dooley felt another shiver and quickly turned right, already looking ahead for any signs of interference. His radio suddenly burst into life, the Chief's voice crackling a couple of inches from his ear. Dooley froze as his chest sprang to life like a trampoline.

"Dooley, you get lost out there?"

"Just got here, Chief," he answered, rubbing his chest as if calming his heart.

"Hurry it up and then head to Mrs. Crowley's. One of her dogs got into the neighbor's yard and attacked their rooster again. Jean says it's a circus over there."

"OK, Chief."

Dooley took a deep breath, held it and tried his best to calm himself again. He peered down at the tombstones, this time trying his best to ignore those with photos on them, the ghosts of those that lay beneath his feet staring back.

When he reached the final tombstone in the row, it sat a few spots from the end, the plots nothing more than a stretch of lawn. The grave before him appeared just as he had expected, the headstone looking almost pristine, despite the harsh weather. There was a fresh bunch of flowers laying across the foot of the marker. Dooley knelt to see pink lilies.

Other than the clean marker, there was nothing that jumped out as being out of place. The grass that had been cut and placed atop the dirt, like a well-fitted rug, appeared just as it should. The young officer felt saddened as he stared into the eyes of the man laying beneath his feet and that's when he froze.

The photo on the headstone suddenly chilled him to the core. Because it wasn't the photo of the man he'd seen back at the station. The man he'd seen on the computer monitor was a man in his 70s, almost completely bald and with bright blue eyes. The man staring back at him looked more in his 30s, with a thick mop of black hair and dark eyes to match. Dooley reached forward to touch the image and as his fingertips ran across its surface, the image moved, held on by a thin film of adhesive.

Dooley stared into the eyes of a stranger and knew there was more to the mystery than he first thought. But was it a simple case of someone simply changing the photo on the headstone? Some kids maybe? The heaviness in his stomach answered the question for him and he reached up to grab his microphone.

"Chief?" he said with a faltering voice.

"What is it, Dooley?"

"I think we have a problem."

Despite the Chief arriving graveside just 15 minutes later, the cemetery proprietor took another hour once Dooley's boss made the call. After confirming what his youngest constable had discovered, Chief Watkins gave the order to have the grave dug up, closing the cemetery for the day in the process.

Dooley attended the gate and ran the yellow police tape across it, cordoning it off from prying eyes. It was a Tuesday afternoon and being one of Danville's smaller cemeteries, meant less chance of anyone dropping by in the foul weather.

Once the respective people finally showed up, the rest of the process happened with relative efficiency and within an hour, two men were standing in an open grave, both kneeling down and rubbing the final bits of dirt from the top of the coffin.

As Chief Watkins, Dooley and Frank Potts stood around the rim watching on, one of the diggers looked up for the go ahead. Chief Watkins looked at the other two men then slowly nodded his head. The man bent down, unsnapped the clasp, then slowly pulled the top half of the lid open.

The men watching all gasped in unison as a face stared out from the coffin's velour interior. It was the man in the picture Dooley had first spotted stuck to the headstone, with one small exception. A neat round bullet hole sat in the middle of his forehead, a faint ring of blood encircling it, as if highlighting its center.

"OK, close it up," the Chief said, hoping to preserve as much evidence as he could. The man standing over the coffin did, his partner carefully climbing out ahead of him. Dooley grabbed the plastic tarpaulin the caregiver had brought with him and once the men had climbed out of the grave, began to cover the hole.

"Head back to the station and call the Maine detectives, Dooley. We need to get Mr. Johns back and figure out what the hell is going on here." The Chief looked at his young constable with sympathetic eyes, remembering that it was still the kid's first week. Dooley nodded, reaching for his keys with trembling fingers, a little thankful to be heading back to base.

It took another two days to bring everything together, during which time Chief Watkins paid the unfortunate widow a visit. He elected to perform the task alone, thinking that a more personal visit might lessen the shock of the situation. He was unsure of just how Nathanial Johns' wife would take the news of her husband taking a final trip out to Maine.

At first, the grieving widow was unsure of whether to believe the man sitting in her living room. The grief still gripped her tightly most days, the relationship she'd had with her husband of 44 years a uniquely close one. His death came suddenly and unannounced, leaving Doris Johns in shock for nearly a week before trying to come to terms with the tragedy.

But to learn that Nathanial had somehow managed to travel almost a thousand miles when he should have been enjoying his eternal rest, was nothing short of frightening for her. Chief Watkins didn't need to show her the photo he'd brought along for comparison, the many frames dotting the walls of the home already featuring the man in question.

"May I ask when you visited your husband last, Mrs. Johns?" Brody Watkins asked, reaching for the cup his host had sat before him.

"I haven't found it easy to go out there. I don't drive, you see?" She sipped her own cup as Brody set his back down. "Why do you ask?" He thought of the flowers Dooley had pointed out, the fresh bunch of lilies placed on the grave.

"Just curious. Trying to get a sense of time. Could you tell me if there's anyone else that would visit him? Children, friends, anyone who cared for him?"

Doris looked at him and offered up a gentle smile. She took another drink from her cup and Brody could see her struggling with the fresh grief of her loss.

"I'm really sorry to put you through this. I just have to establish what happened." He tried his best to sound empathic.

"Nathanial and I didn't have children, Chief. Our only son passed many years ago. We mostly kept to ourselves, especially during the past few years. We tried to live a quiet life for the most part. The only time we really ventured anywhere was to the west coast of Florida once a year."

Brody nodded and asked a few more non-official questions in an effort to change the mood of the conversation. It worked for the most part, Doris giving him a brief glimpse into the back room of the home where Nathanial's model trains still lived.

He nodded and listened as she explained her late husband's hobby, talking with an air of affection that only served to weigh heavier on the conversation. Once they headed back out to the kitchen, Brody finished his tea, thanked the widow and returned to his cruiser, the questions continuing to build in his mind.

It took almost another week before the Danville Police Department could put a name to the second part of their mystery. After a chance discovery by a holidaying constable, the name Eugene Garcia was finally linked to the John Doe currently residing in one of the morgue storage units.

The constable had been on a weekend getaway with his new fiancé to Richmond, Virginia. It was whilst enjoying a local newspaper with his breakfast that he came across the small column about a missing person. The photo of the missing man was quite small, but Leonard Parker instantly recognized the face. By the time he was eating dinner that night, the missing man had been positively confirmed as being that of the stranger back in Danville.

But while the identification of the man had been accomplished, the answers to their many questions continued to elude the investigating officers. They had a man purposefully taken almost a thousand miles from his grave to some backwater in Maine, while another had been executed and buried in his stead. None of it made sense and despite putting in many man hours, the investigation stalled before it had even begun.

The late Nathanial Johns was eventually returned to his final resting place, a grateful Doris attending the second burial of her husband in almost as many weeks. The process was difficult, but when it was over with, she returned to the home she had shared with him for the better part of 30 years, a place where she felt closest to him.

As for Eugene Garcia, the answers remained as mysterious as the rest of the events leading up to the discovery of his body. Because he was a single man, living a bachelor life with very few friends, the only information the officers were able to obtain were from his sister. But it had been several years since she'd seen her brother, having moved to Montreal with her husband and children.

As far as the pieces they managed to put together, Garcia had been a closet homosexual, unable to fully admit his lifestyle to either his family or the few friends he had, most of whom were little more than workplace acquaintances. The man worked as a shoe salesman, had a clean record and didn't appear to have any vices, such as drugs or alcohol. As far as anyone could tell, the man was a loner, a clean skin and a simple law abiding citizen.

While the authorities desperately tried to follow any possible clues before they went cold, they were unaware that another organization had taken an interest in the case, one far more inconspicuous than any they'd heard of before. It was the kind of agency that took matters of murder into their own hands, to solve the crimes and end the killings, much like a vigilante mob might track down a local perpetrator. And when this agency identified the true culprit, nothing would save them from the executioner's punishment.

Purchase Body Switch now and continue your journey with Sam Rader in Book 2

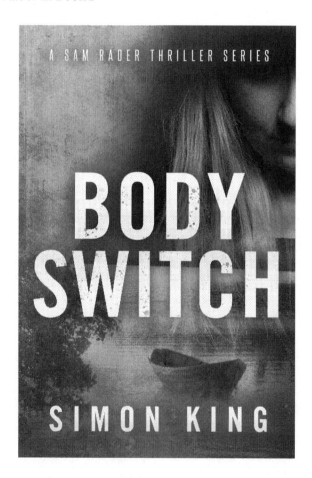

A LETTER FROM JUDITH

The following letter is one sent from Samantha's mom and answers some very important questions if you haven't yet read The Lawson Chronicles. While this is a separate series from that one and can be read on its own merits, it does owe its existence to the horror that occurred more than half a century ago, during the time of Harry Lightman and the events that begin with The Final Alibi.

PART 1

Dear Sammi,

We are killers. There I said it. I know you've been wondering about your past, and my past as well, but for all this time, I couldn't answer your questions. I totally understand the struggles you face on a daily basis, because like you, I also carry the demons inside me. The demons, those damn demons.

I need you to understand why we both carry them with us; why we can never outrun them and why, after all these years, I'm finally giving in. Yes, I'm giving in. I can no longer deal with the events that unfolded during the days I spent with that monster. In a way, I guess you're the lucky one, the first since my mother to have a life without directly knowing Harry Lightman. Because he is the evil in our past.

Harry Lightman was your great-grandfather. He was also a prolific serial killer, responsible for somewhere in the area of four dozen murders, although authorities say it's closer to five. He wrote about the early years of his life in a diary, which he wrote for a man called Jim Lawson, my adopted uncle. It was

Jim and my mom, your grandma, that hunted Lightman after he murdered my carer and abducted me.

While Grandma and Jim eventually found him, and Grandma 'took care' of him, it was during those days in his company that I witnessed some pretty horrific things, things I've never shared with anybody. I didn't think there was a need, especially with both Lightman and Grandma long gone. While Jim did try a couple of times to speak to me about those events, he also respected my wishes not to talk about them. I was just a kid back then and honestly figured the nightmares would simply vanish into the realms of forgotten-hood.

But they didn't. The memories became recurring night-mares for me, continuing to this very day. There's no outrun-ning those kinds of experiences, no matter how much you try. All the counseling in the world couldn't help. Yes, there were drugs prescribed to me, and a few of the 'under-the-counter' varieties, but none helped me deal with the horror still running loose around my mind.

For me, there's only one solution left and I wanted to explain things before you found out from someone else. No one knows what happened during those days, because I don't want the knowledge to spread. I thought that if I hung on to it, then I could somehow keep the evil locked away from the world.

But this evil is the kind that refuses to die. It's like an angry presence that relentlessly wears away the walls of confinement, until it eventually finds its way back out. So now, I'll hand it to you via this letter, in the hope that you simply burn it, to finally rid the world of Harry Lightman. But if you do chose to read on, to find out once and for all about the evils that coarse through your veins, then understand I won't be able to help you.

I contemplated not writing this and simply taking them to my grave. But I didn't want you struggling for the rest of your life, wondering about why you have such evil thoughts, urges that were directly passed from Lightman, through me, to you. I guess, in a way, I'm to blame for your struggles.

I didn't want a child for that very reason, but I love your father and couldn't continue seeing the sadness in his eyes. He wanted a child more than anyone I've ever known. He would often tell me his plans for the lucky baby that would hopefully one day bless our home. I couldn't bring myself to crushing his dream, so after a lot of soul searching, I finally gave in.

There's no need for me to explain what happened because, well, here you are. But I began to worry when I started noticing your fascination with things that children shouldn't realize. The way you spoke about death and killing from such an early age. Then there's the dead animals you would find and bring home.

One of those memories I have of you is when we went for a walk along old Cutter Lane, back when you were about 5 years old. Do you remember that place? Up in the mountains, near the cabin? Your father was out hunting and I decided to walk along the ridge, out overlooking the lake.

It was along that track that you found the dead rabbit. It was still quite fresh, maybe taken by some predator and dropped when scared off by us. I hadn't noticed the corpse as we walked past, but you did. When I turned to see where you were and found you almost 50 yards behind me, bent over something, I had no idea what you were doing.

But when I came back and saw what you'd found, I just about screamed in horror. It scared the shit out of me, Sammie. You were kneeling down, a glazed look in your eyes and you had ripped some of the rabbit's insides out. One of your hands was deep inside its cavity, while the other you kind of held out a little, covered in fresh blood.

The horror of seeing you do that brought back every fear I'd had before your birth. Right there at that moment, I honestly thought I'd given birth to a new serial killer, like Lightman reincarnated. He is inside you, after all. Good old Pop.

There was nothing I could do, but stand there and stare in terror, unable to move, while you performed a dissection on the rabbit's entrails. It was when you shushed a fly from your face with a bloodied hand and left a streak of blood along your cheek that I finally screamed. I picked you up, scolded you like never before and turned for home.

The look of surprise on your face was one I've never forgotten. You had no idea why I was yelling at you. It was as if you'd been innocently playing with your toys and I had simply lost the plot. I don't know whether you remember that day; I hope you don't, but I doubt it. Shit like that aways manages to keep hanging on.

I guess to really convey just what happened, I have to go back, back to the very beginning. It's not something that comes easy to me because, well, I've tried my hardest to block everything out as best I could. While certain highlights still plague me, and have forever, the details are lost in a fog that's almost impenetrable. It's as if I'm watching the scenes play out through a misted window and yet the details of those scenes appear foreign.

I'm sorry, sweetheart. I know it makes no sense whatsoever. But somehow I need to get this out once and for all. So you can finally learn of our family heritage and the horrific events that played out before you were born. One last chance to burn this shit?

"Uba", as she liked me to call her, was my nanny before the events began. She was our neighbor back then and would often come and watch me while momma was at work. Uba was one of the most kind-hearted people I have ever known in my life.

There were so many wonderful things she would show me, but the best was her drawing. Uba was an amazing artist and it was her I gained my own skill in drawing from. Thankfully, it is one of the better qualities I passed on to you.

She would often try and bestow other things on me, like cooking and laundry work, but it was the drawing I took to the most. We would draw for hours, often comparing our finished pieces with each other. My favorite thing to draw were horses and I would spend an entire afternoon on a single piece. It was during one of those pieces that life changed forever, leaving me with scars deep enough to engrave my soul and which left my beautiful Uba dead.

I still remember the knock on the door as if it was yesterday. It was the kind of knock that intrigued more than startled, because it wasn't a very loud one, just hard enough to bring about a touch of curiosity. Uba went and answered that knock while I remained at the kitchen table, my pencils surrounding me in all directions. Uba had a thing for pastels and they were intermingled with my own colored utensils.

There was a quiet muffled conversation from the hallway and when Uba returned to the kitchen with the stranger standing behind her, she had a nervous look on her face, one that at first I thought meant something had happened to momma.

"Go and sit in your room for a bit, Jude," Uba told me and the man gave a slight nod. He didn't smile, just stared at me with a kind of vacant stare.

Once the door was closed to my room, I simply sat on my bed and waited for them to discuss what they needed to. More muffled conversation followed, but there were no sounds of a struggle, not that I heard anyway. After several minutes, the house grew silent and I sat on that bed with the butterflies feeling uncomfortable in my belly.

Finally, the door slowly swung open and I half sat up, expecting Uba to pop her head through and ask me back into the kitchen. But it wasn't her face that looked in at me. It was the stranger that had stood behind Uba as she told me to sit in my room. That stranger now peered in through the open door, silently watching me with a weird grin.

Without speaking, he slowly walked into my bedroom, watching me as he did. Once he stood near my dresser, he reached up and took a photo from the wall, opened the frame and retrieved the picture. He then took a new one from his pocket and looked at it for a bit. As if remembering I was there, he held the photo up for me to see.

"Don't they look like a lovely family?" he asked, grinning at me again. But that was when I saw something that instantly chilled me. There was a smear on the side of his mouth; something red and shiny. Of course now I know it was Uba's blood, but back then, I thought it was tomato ketchup. "You see this little girl here?" he continued, pointing at a young blond girl that was held in her mother's arms. "You're going to meet her soon. Would you like that, Jude? Maybe meet a new friend?"

There was a nervous twitch in my eye and although I nodded at him, felt terrified as I sat there feeling completely helpless. I wished for momma, but she was away with work, helping Jim with something.

"Where's Uba?" I asked and he ignored me, simply slid the new photo into place, snapped the back where it belonged and then carefully hung the frame back on the wall.

"Uba has gone to where all the other great nannies live." He turned to me, standing only a few feet from my bed. "Time to go and meet your new friend," he said. But I had no intention of going with him, so instead jumped and ran from the room.

He was slow off the mark, but within a second, I heard his footfalls almost directly behind me.

The kitchen was only a few feet from my bedroom door, but Uba wasn't in there. With Lightman right behind me, I did a circle around the table, then raced into the living room. I saw Uba's feet lying on the ground and froze. The coffee table mostly blocked the top half of her from my sight and as I stepped to one side to see why she was lying still, felt a searing pain as my hair was ripped to one side.

The lights went out as something exploded into the side of my face. I think he punched me, because the next thing I knew, we were driving along some country road, the radio quietly playing in the background. I'll never forget the song that played as I woke, because it had been our favorite, momma often playing it really loud while her and I danced. It was Patti Page singing "How much is that doggy in the window".

But there would be no more dancing for us after that day. Not for Uba and certainly not for momma and I. Our dancing days were over, thanks to Lightman. Everyone's lives were about to change, courtesy of that arsehole.

He didn't see me wake at first. I was lying across the back seat and as I came to, became aware of where I was almost immediately. I saw the door and meant to open it and jump out. But I was scared. The trees we were passing were visible through the far window and as I watched them, thought he was driving into the country to do away with me.

But then I remembered Uba and began to cry. That was when he heard me. Lightman turned and looked at me. But the look I was expecting to see was gone. There was a kindness in his eyes, like sorrow almost.

"Hey there. Finally awake?"

SIMON KING

We drove for what felt like hours, the only sounds coming from the hum of the tires and the faint tunes from the radio. He'd turned back to look at me occasionally, but these were brief and rare. At one point, Lightman handed me a jar of biscuits and I saw that they were from our kitchen counter. Uba had baked them just the day before.

Despite not wanting any, my hunger deceived me and I was soon munching on one, with another held in my other hand.

"These are damn good. Must have been a real wiz in the kitchen, that nannie of yours," he said, chewing on one. I didn't answer, just glaring at him as I ate the food. "I remember my mom used to bake biscuits. Not as good as these though."

Once I finished the biscuits, I laid back down on the seat and closed my eyes. I didn't want to see the world. I didn't want to hear the world. It needed to be blocked out and I tried as hard as I could. But then he started whistling, a weird sort of tune that I didn't recognize. I now know it to be Fur Elise, the melody following me into my nightmares even today.

Lightman suddenly pulled the car over and stopped. Only once I'd sat up did I notice that we were on a dirt road, although road was probably an overstatement. It looked more like a track at best and Lightman had parked under a nest of trees to one side of it. There were birds singing overhead, but apart from that, no other sounds of any type of life could be heard.

"Come on. We walk from here," he said, swinging his door open. When I didn't move straight away, he opened my door and reached in, grabbing me by the hair. The hot pain shot through my head and I tried my best to climb out. "Know what I hate?" he snarled into my face as he lent down to my level. "Repeating myself."

The track was on the side of a hill and I could see out across a valley beneath us. There were several paddocks lined up like a chess board, stretching all the way across to the other side of the expanse, until another set of hills cut them off. Some of those fields were freshly worked, the deep brown of overturned earth staring back. I think that was the smell that hung in the air as well, although I can't be sure.

"Let's go," Lightman grunted and began to walk back towards the way we'd driven.

"Where are we going?" I asked.

"To catch up with an old friend," he cackled and the sound of it sent shivers through me. He was evil, I knew that from the onset. There was a sense of death that hung over him like a veil and was only too aware that he would kill me if I became too much of a nuisance.

He didn't slow, just continuing to walk, all the while whistling the same tune, over and over. The sound of that tune was maddening and I plugged my ears up at one point. When Lightman turned back to make sure I was following, he laughed when he saw my fingers pressed firmly into my ears.

"What's the matter? My whistling not up to standard?" he asked and again I ignored him. It didn't seem to bother him and we continued walking to what I would soon find to be the most horrific experience of my life.

"There he is," Lightman said as he surveyed the valley below. We'd been walking for almost an hour and had turned off the track at one point. He led me through some pretty thick under-brush, but we eventually came out on top of a hill that over-looked another large valley. There were maybe 3 or 4 farm houses dotted across the landscape and he pointed at one of them.

"There's who?" I asked him.

"Someone who should have known when to leave shit alone," he whispered into the sky. "Ever had a bully in your life, Jude?" I just shook my head, not sure of the meaning. Lightman considered me for a second, then nodded. "Well, you might one day. Most people come across those arseholes at some point. He was one of mine. Just one of them. Made my life a fucking nightmare. Anyway, I've come to repay the favor."

We began walking again, slowly making our way down the side of the hill. Once near the road, Lightman checked for traffic before crossing, carefully eyeing off the farmhouse now before us. There was a dust cloud a couple of fields behind the house and Lightman seemed to pay it as much attention as the home.

Just before we reached the main drive leading up to the house, my kidnapper stopped and knelt down in my face.

"I'm only gonna say this once, kid. Keep your trap shut, you hear me? Otherwise you'll wish you were one of them by the time I finish with you." He didn't have to repeat himself. I knew perfectly well what he meant and had no intention of heading down that path.

Once he was sure I understood, he rose back up and took my hand. I was expecting his touch to feel cold, almost icy, but instead found his hand warm.

"Let's go," he said, leading me on towards my first experience of the Daylesford Devil.

When we reached the front door of the farmhouse, Lightman winked at me one final time, then put one finger to his lips.

"Remember what I said," he whispered, then knocked on the door. There was movement in the home and a few moments later a woman opened the door to us.

"Can I help you?" she asked. I remember her eyes looking so warm and friendly.

"Hello. My daughter and I broke down just up the road and we were hoping to use your telephone. If you have one of course."

The woman eyed him suspiciously, looking from me to him and back again. Then she offered us a smile that matched her eyes and invited us inside. The rest of the house sat quietly behind her and I thought about the other kids I'd seen in that photo.

The mom led us into a kitchen and pointed to where the phone hung on the wall. She was about to say something else when a girl poked her head through the doorway.

"Momma?"

"This is my Jasmine." The mom looked at me and smiled. "Jassie? Why don't you show this little girl your new dollhouse?"

The woman didn't know it, but she played right into Lightman's hands. Once Jasmine and I were in her room, Harry overpowered Mrs Thompson and took her out into one of the sheds. I didn't see this happen of course, but he came to the bedroom shortly after and told us to stay in the room, before closing us in. Jasmine Thompson was OK, to begin with, happily playing dolls with me. But then she started asking for her mom and pretty soon opened the door.

Lightman told me to stay in the room and shut me inside again. He must have taken the girl out to see her mom and also tied her up, the way he would also tie the boys up less than an hour later when they returned from whatever exploring boys tend to get up to.

By the time Reedy Thompson came home from working

the fields, his family were strung up and waiting for their moment with Lucifer. The poor father never saw the attack coming, Lightman waiting behind a door. All I heard was the crack of something hitting a dull object and then the crash of it hitting the ground.

I opened the door to see and saw the man lying on the ground, blood seeping from an open wound on his head. Lightman grabbed me first and tied my hands up before leading me out into the shed. That was the first time I saw the family, all tied and hanging from their wrists, each with a gag in their mouth.

The horror I saw in their eyes is something I have carried with me forever, Sammie. They had no clue about why they were there, or what was about to happen. The mom was crying uncontrollably, begging for her children's lives. Beside her, Jasmine was sobbing, looking up at her mother with a look of deep-seated fear.

Lightman tied me to a post and told me to wait, as if I could somehow wander around. He then returned to the main house and was gone for a long time. The four of them kept staring at me, the mom trying desperately to say something. But the gag did its job and we simply stared at each other across the expanse of the shed.

After listening to some kind of hammering coming from the home, Lightman finally returned, dragging the unconscious father into the shed on a chair. At first I thought he'd tied him to it, but soon saw the nails sticking out from his hands.

I began to scream, drowning out the desperate cries of the family now staring at their protector all but incapacitated. They were all vulnerable to whatever evil Lightman had planned. Little did I know that it would begin with me.

He came and stood right in front of me until I stopped screaming, then knelt down until his face was in mine.

"They say you are my granddaughter. If that is true, then you already have the same shit in you that's running through me. The same bad that has crippled me my whole life must be in you as well. Ready to find out?"

Lightman untied me and dragged me to the father. He was still unconscious, although at the time, I was sure he was dead. There was so much blood on him that there was no way he was still alive. That was when Harry took a knife out and pointed it at his former tormentor.

"See how his eyes are shut? I don't think he should miss a single thing. What do you think?" Before I had a chance to answer, Lightman carefully pulled on one of the man's eyelids, then sliced it off with his blade.

That was when the man starting coming too, a low grunt building into a morbid groan. Lightman didn't pause, slicing the other eyelid off with little apprehension. As if to ensure the man was waking, he stabbed the blade's point into his cheek.

"Awake, cunt?"

I wish I could say the horror offended me. I wanted it to. But Lightman was right. There was something inside me that felt, well, bad. And worse than that, he could see it as well. He knew what I was thinking and recognized what it really meant. The moment our eyes locked, he knew who I really was.

He dragged me to one of the boys, grabbed his knife and cut the sleeve off the kid's jumper. He spoke to me as if no-one else was around, completely ignoring the muffled screams of the family around us.

That was the first time he bit any of them. He watched me as he did it, the kid passing out as Lightman's teeth sunk into his flesh. The mother lost control of her bladder and the other boy just stared wide eyed. I think he pissed himself as well, although I can't be sure.

All I remember was staring as Lightman tore a piece of meat from that kid's arm and then chewed as if he'd taken a bite out of a hamburger. Behind us, the father was howling, screaming at Lightman to stop; begging him to let his family go.

But no-one was leaving that shed untouched. Not with the vengeance he had in store. Lightman held the arm out to me, wanting me to follow suit. I'm not sure if I screamed, but I do remember vomiting. His laughter filled my ears as I doubled over.

When I was finished, he dragged me to Jasmine. The mother was crying and I think she knew at that point. She knew that Lightman was going to kill them all. It was the way her fight had gone out of her screams, instead turning into a low weeping.

The first boy started to come around again and began to shake uncontrollably while groaning. The father was still screaming abuse towards us, but Lightman wasn't listening. He was focused only on me, and the little girl standing before us.

Pulling me closer, he grabbed the sleeve of her jumper and tore it away, then pushed me towards her.

"Your turn," he whispered to me. I tried to pull away, I really did. Despite feeling that badness inside, I struggled my hardest against it. He kept pulling me closer, at one point grabbing a handful of hair. The pain exploded from the back of my head and I felt his spittle hit me as he yelled for me to show him how much I was his granddaughter.

Jasmine Thompson screamed as Lightman pushed my face closer towards her. We were both crying and I tried to stop, to pull back. But he was so much stronger than I was and I knew I stood little chance.

"Bite this bitch or I kill you first," he snarled at me and

something inside me just snapped. I don't know whether it was fear or pain or something else, but all I remember is the warmth of her blood as my teeth took hold.

The screams that followed became an intertwined mass of tortured souls, but for me, none of it mattered. Because as soon as I felt the warm blood run down my throat, my legs finally gave out and I lost consciousness.

PART 2

T he next thing I knew, we were driving again, but this time in a different car, one I instantly recognized. I recognized it because there was a teddy bear sticking out from under one of the seats. It was my teddy bear and the car was my mom's.

I don't remember how we came to be in the car, but I do remember the smell, because it wasn't how the car normally smelled. It was a rank odor, almost metallic. It filled the car's cabin and I knew it was blood.

You have to remember that I was quite young during this time, Sammie. Some memories remain, while others have faded out completely with the passage of time. Thankfully, not everything remained inside my head, but there was enough to keep the nightmare going for a long time.

I don't remember how long we drove for, but at some point, Harry began talking to me. It was dark outside, so I had very little idea of where we were headed, not that I would have known anyway. He said I had shown great promise and I may yet live to see my mother again. Apparently, taking a chunk out of Jasmine Thompson was enough to keep me alive a while longer.

Along the way to wherever we were headed, he began to explain his own childhood and all the people that had hurt him. He was not only bullied by a lot of the townsfolk, but also 'buggered' by a couple of the 'damn pigs' that were supposed to protect him, although I didn't understand what that meant. Not at the time anyway.

It was only once I was older that the words returned to me and I understood what he'd meant. In a way, I can understand how Lightman became the person he did. It must have been horrible to put up with what he had.

He also told me about his own momma having been killed by his father. I mean, the man watched his mother die right before his eyes. Can you imagine? I mean, the terror he must have gone through.

I'm starting to sound like I'm defending him, aren't I? That's not my intention, believe me. That prick was a sick fuck who killed a lot of people, some of which I got to witness. Like the woman we went to see after the Thompson family.

After driving for another couple of hours, he finally pulled over and parked in an abandoned farm shed. After making sure the car was well out of view, he locked me in the trunk and told me to sleep. Said he needed to get some shuteye himself so he was refreshed for the ultimate payback. I did as he asked and remember the fear as I listened to the noises from outside.

A lot of that night disappeared with time and the next thing I remember was when he cracked the trunk's lid and blinding sunshine hit my eyes. I'd been sleeping and was startled awake.

Lightman's smile was the first think I saw and it's something I still see to this day.

After helping me out of the car, he opened the back door and told me to get in. Said he had to make a phone call. I don't know who he needed to speak to, but he stopped at a cafe in some small town about 20 minutes down the road.

After dialing the number and waiting a few seconds, he began to speak. But the name he said first is what pricked my ears.

"Ah, Officer Connor," was what he said and I felt myself get all sweaty with fear. I don't know why, but I think it was the thought of knowing my mom was on the other end of that line.

He suddenly held the phone down to me and said I should speak with her. I remember him holding the receiver to my ear. There was a grin on his face, looking more menacingly than ever.

"Baby?" she whispered and I began to cry. "Stay strong, pumpkin. Momma will come for you soon. You just stay strong." He pulled the receiver back, said something else to her, then hung up.

Shortly after, we were back in the car, eating ham and cheese sandwiches and drinking cokes. I wasn't hungry, but I knew he wasn't going to take no for an answer. Part of me thought he'd arranged to meet my mom, but the next person he went to see was a man called Leon something. He was an old man, his long white beard stained yellow from cigarette smoke. The man kept looking at me as Lightman spoke to him and after a brief exchange, invited us in.

The man had a small dog and I sat with it in the living room as the men talked about something. At one point, Harry told me to sit tight and not move, while him and the other man disappeared. I think Harry killed him then and stuffed his body into the trunk of his car.

We stayed at that house for a day, I think. Maybe even 2, I don't remember. But when we left again, it wasn't in my mom's car, but the old man's. Harry made me sit in the back, while he drove, whistling his standard tone. Every now and then he'd begin to laugh, a deep low chuckle that sounded gruesome.

After a few hours of driving, we started to see a lot of traffic and Harry told me that we would soon stop. When we did, I had to join our passenger in the trunk, but only for a little while. He needed to take care of some important business and couldn't have me under his feet.

"He's just sleeping, that's all," he chuckled, looking at me.

When he stopped at a park, we sat for almost an hour, while he seemed to watch for something. There were some cookies in a plastic bag Harry had brought and he handed me one, telling me to eat so I wouldn't be hungry while keeping an eye on our passenger.

"Right on time," he said at one point, staring out through the windshield and I sat up to see what he'd spotted. There was a row of houses and parked in front of one was a police car. 2 officers were climbing out and Harry seemed to have a vested interest in them, barely blinking as he watched them.

We continued to sit in the car and after some time, he made another weird noise as he kept watching. I looked and saw as an old lady and the 2 officers walked down the road and entered a church. The building was only a couple of hundred yards away and I could see their faces clearly. Once they were inside, Harry smiled, then slowly chuckled.

"Almost time."

It was almost 2 hours later that I was finally told to follow him out of the car. I did and when he opened the trunk, saw the old man lying inside. Thankfully, he was facing towards the corner, almost curled up as he lay still to one side.

"Just asleep," Harry repeated. I had a thought of just running, but knew he'd catch me, even if I started screaming. And then there was the thought of my mom. What if he'd hurt her because of me?

I did as he told me and climbed into the trunk. A second later I was in darkness, scared beyond stiff. There was a dead man lying next to me and a killer standing just outside. I think that was when I wet myself, I don't quite remember.

I do know that there wasn't a lot of noise. Not until I heard Harry say something like, "Oh, there you are, James," or something similar. A few moments later, the car door opened, then slammed shut, leaving me in silence once more.

Time must have passed so slowly, because I had no sense of it at all. It was just a horrendous period of time as I lay perfectly still, waiting for the old man to reach out to me. I was sure he would. I could have sworn I heard him move at one point, a deathly scraping as his arm slowly etched closer, his fingers probing to find me.

The smell was horrible, almost filling the trunk with a sickly heaviness of shit. It wasn't until years later that I learned people's bowels let go after death. That was the smell from the trunk that day. That was the stench I had to endure while lying next to a corpse, waiting for death to reach out to me.

Something jolted the car then, followed by a bang as the door slammed shut. The trunk lid suddenly opened and Harry's hand reached in, grabbing me painfully by the arm.

"What the fuck?" he muttered. "Piss yourself?" He pushed me towards the car door and I climbed in. He followed and sat down again, watching intently for something. It was already dark and I couldn't see a lot. But shortly after, he seemed to cheer a little, then started the car and drove a little way further along the park.

Once he stopped, he got out briefly, did something at the back of the car then closed the trunk lid. Once back inside, he slammed the door shut and revved the car hard. It lurched forward as Harry began to cheer loudly. I didn't know what he'd done, but whatever it was, he didn't stop laughing and cheering for a long time.

We drove for a few more hours and I think I slept again at some point. I was awoken by Harry grabbing my arm and pulling me out of the car again. Although it looked as if it was night still, I soon realized that we were parked inside a garage of some sort.

I honestly don't remember how long we'd been there, but as Harry led me inside the main house, there was a man tied up in what looked like a very small kitchen, lying on the floor with his hands bound behind him. His eyes were terrified and he had blood weeping from the side of his head, his mouth gagged with what looked like a tea towel.

"Ever met a copycat before?" Harry said to me, before taking me through to the bathroom. He told me I could clean myself up once we'd finished with the other man. There was a pair of pants and a shirt sitting on the edge of the sink and despite being a little big, I couldn't wait to put them on after a shower. I didn't know it then, but that was the man I would kill.

As the man continued to struggle on the ground, Harry prepared me a sandwich, which I ate standing in the kitchen.

He kept kicking the man every so often, as if waking him up each time he passed him. There was a real hatred from Harry towards him, even worse than the others we'd already dealt with.

"Know why you have clothes that fit you?" Harry asked me as I finished my food. "Because Jeremy here, likes to hurt little children. He also likes to pretend that he's me, don't you?" He kicked him in the face, the unfortunate man yelping in pain.

I stood there watching, horrified at what was to come. Harry suddenly grabbed the man, knelt down and buried his face in the man's neck. They began to wrestle, with the tied up man screeching in horror. It was far from what he was about to endure.

As Harry stood up again, he spat something out as I saw a hole in the man's throat. There was blood pouring from the wound and that's when Harry reached inside the front of the man's pants. There was another struggle, his face turned pale and I think he passed out as Harry removed his hand covered in more blood.

I don't need to go into all the specifics, Sammie. I think you get the idea. He fed that man's testicles to his dog. I know, because he announced it as he called the pooch over. After he was done, Harry pulled me towards the man and held out his arm to me. I think I was as pale as he was, my legs feeling barely able to hold me up.

But Harry soon fixed that, pushing me down on the ground and holding the arm out. Jeremy Winters came to again and looked up at me with pure terror in his eyes.

"Start or I'll make you do this to your mother."

I did as I was told, a mix of tears, vomit and endless retching filling the room. While the man continued to struggle wildly against his bindings, there was nothing he could do. He was as much a prisoner as I was. There was no escape for either one of us.

Soon after, the struggles slowly began to subside as the blood loss and trauma stole his life away. I didn't know at the time, but the man we were killing was also a murderer. He'd been using Harry's killing method for himself, hiding in the shadows of Lucifer.

Once Winters was dead, Harry finally let me go, telling me to wash up. I must have stood in that shower for a long time, the hot water feeling so soothing. Once I was dressed in the new clothes, I returned to the kitchen, but Winters was gone. Harry tied my hands up and then tied me to the kitchen table. Said he had to clean himself up.

Once he returned, he wrote something on a bit of paper, which he stuffed into his shirt pocket. Then we jumped in the car and drove to a place where Harry took the body. He told me afterwards that it was the man's shop. My mom and Jim Lawson would find him the very next day.

PART 3

The horror I endured during those days is something that I have never been able to escape from. While Harry may have thought of me as being one of his kind, I was anything but. The 'badness' I felt during those days isn't something I've shared with anyone. A large part of me continues to believe that maybe there is a side of me that could turn into what he'd become. Maybe he was right. Maybe badness and evil does get passed from one generation to the next. Maybe I really was supposed to follow in his footsteps. But despite all the help I have been offered, there is nothing that can ever take the horrific memories away.

There was more death after Jeremy Winters, but those are mostly forgotten. The only other death that I can still truly remember is my mom, the one that really mattered the most. That moment still plays out whenever the lights go out. The smell of the wood chips; the sounds of the mill; the sound of that chipper brought to life. I still see her face as she ran at that psycho, giving me a final glance just before she hit him. I'm not sure, but in my mind I see a tear roll down her cheek. She also appeared to mouth something. I'm sure it was the words 'I love you' but I can't be sure.

And then there's that God-awful sound when they both fell into the chipper, the scream of grinding metal temporarily dulled as the teeth became lubricated with their blood. Lightman did try to yell out some kind of objection, but those words were cut off just like his head was, lost in a flood of gore.

A man named Darren Fermaner came to help us. I think my mom was supposed to kill him, along with Jim and I, but she saved them. She saved all of us that night. There's a small wooden box in my bedside chest. Inside you'll find a medal. It's a bravery medal the police gave me after her death. I guess it's a small piece of light from a darkness best left forgotten.

The people you know as Grandma and Grandpa are not your biological grandparents. Grandpa worked in the prison where Harry Lightman was kept and it was Jim Lawson that met him and his wife while trying to find me. Those were some very grim days and once everything had settled and I had nowhere to go, they were his choice to be my guardians.

They were such an amazingly warm couple and gave me a real home. Things should have been perfect, but of course they weren't. The endless nightmares that kept me awake at night took a toll on everybody. Even Jim eventually stopped coming. I couldn't blame him of course. The distances and costs were astronomical and he had his own life to live.

Sometimes I think that visiting me brought a lot of his own bad memories back. The man had lost his own mom during those terrifying days. She was the one Harry murdered while I was stuck in the trunk with the dead man. Given his own loss, I understand what seeing me must have meant for him.

Despite moving half way around the world and the psycho long since dead, life should have taken on some sort of normality for me. Grandma and Grandpa certainly tried their best. But the evil I witnessed during those days somehow remained inside me. I could feel it, Sammie; the 'badness' still lying dormant inside me.

There were times where I was sure it would rise to the surface, almost feeling it starting to bubble as my own anger rose. And that was what scared me the most. Passing that anger on to my own child. It was very early on that I made the decision not to have children. Whatever evil still lurked inside me, would end with me once and for all. Harry Lightman's legacy would finally crumble, ending with his final heir.

But then I met your father, a man so strong and loving and caring. This might come as a surprise to you, but your father saved my life the first time we met. It was he that talked me off the bridge that fateful day.

My mind had been a mess for several months in the lead up to that moment. There was a lot going on and my anger kept threatening to boil over. I could feel the rage lying there, just waiting for me to finally release it. Eventually, I decided to end things once and for all. My time had come and it was going to be my final day on earth.

The Gorge Bridge was only a few miles from where I was living at the time and seemed like the perfect place. No more problems. That is a high-arsed bridge, kiddo. Standing on the edge of that thing, hanging onto the railing and waiting for you fingers to finally let go is one of life's true eye-opening moments. You'll certainly know if you want to live once you look down to the bottom.

But your father happened to be driving past at that moment. He'd driven down from Denver to visit his mom. She lived in Taos and he later told me he always drove over the bridge. It was like a ritual for him.

There wasn't a lot of traffic at that time of day and his was the first car that came along. I barely heard him, too caught up in preparing to meet my fate at the bottom of that chasm. But he stopped and, before long, managed to convince me that there was more to life than living in the past. "The past is behind you for a reason" was how he put it and do you know what? It made perfect sense at the time.

After taking me home, Samuel Rader insisted on returning time and time again. Grandma would tell me how much that man was smitten with me every time she saw him. I was living in the cottage out back from the main house at the time. This was shortly after Grandpa had died. I wanted to be close to her, but those fucken demons refused to let me be.

It was Samuel that helped me overcome them. He'd had his own demons of course, those he picked up whilst on deployment. He never spoke much about his work, but I knew he was into serious things.

He'd taken me shopping one day and we stopped at a diner for lunch. A group of men began to harass me from the moment we sat down, making derogatory comments about me. Your father remained incredibly calm, even when one flicked a ketchup-covered fry at him.

But then, one of the men made the mistake of standing up and coming to our table. He knelt down close by Samuel's face and whispered something, his friend's watching with shit-eating grins across their faces.

It was when that man patted the top of my head that I first saw what your father was capable of. Four grown men were lying groaning on the diner floor not 30 seconds later. I'd never seen moves like that in real life before and he made it look so easy.

It was your father that eventually convinced me that there was enough good in him to beat any bad that lived inside me. He was desperate for children, but for years I held my promise close to my chest, refusing to give in. I don't know why he stayed with me. He could have had anyone else, someone who'd give him all the babies in the world.

But he refused to leave me, saying that there was a reason it was him that drove along the bridge that day. It was his gentle soul and strong heart that finally won me over to give him a single child; you.

The promise he made that the good in him would dominate any bad in me, inside our baby, held true for a long time. But then I saw you with that damn rabbit and that's when I knew. That's when I realized there was a piece of Harry Lightman inside you, just as it lived inside me.

Despite trying my hardest to beat the nightmares, I can go on no more, kiddo. I'm so sorry. Sometimes I think that maybe, just maybe if I had met Samuel a few years earlier, he may have had a chance to truly save me. But I think too many years had taken their toll on me. The nightmares swirling around my mind had done what they set out to do.

But not you. You have a real chance with such a strong father to help you. He really is the one person who will protect you from all the shit in this world. With me, he really never had a chance. But you, my love, you have his kindness and strength and resilience inside you and that's what is going to keep you safe.

I'm so sorry for giving up. I'm sorry for abandoning you to your fate and leaving you to face this shit on your own. But part of me likes to think that if I can leave early enough, the badness inside you won't have a chance to fully evolve. Maybe it will just whither away and die before it has a chance to completely mature.

You are the very last of our line, Sammie. I pray that your father will have the strength to finally break the evil bonds that have held this family for so long. I know he will keep you safe if you let him. If only I had allowed myself to fully open up to him.

Goodbye my sweet little girl. I hope the badness dies with me and you can live the wonderful life you deserve.

Momma

P.S. Remember. The past is behind you for a reason.

AFTERWORD

So what did you think of the first Sam Rader Thriller? I hope you enjoyed reading it as much as I enjoyed writing it. I have plans for several more books this year in this series and you can order the next right now.

There's something special about Sam that I find intriguing. She didn't have much of a social life growing up and yet, here she is, protecting those that at one point bullied her. It just goes to show that there really is more to one's existence than might be visible at any given point. All it needs is a little different perception.

Thank you again for joining me, I really appreciate your support. And don't forget to join my mailing list at www.booksbysimonking.com for all the exciting news on upcoming releases and other little bits I like to share.

Take care and stay safe.

Simon

July 22nd, 2020

Made in the USA
Middletown, DE
13 December 2023

45601470R00130